To Brooke – so great

Soul Two Soul

Evan Clouse

Wanna go on a trip?

Copyright © 2023 by Evan Clouse.

Library of Congress Control Number: Pending

ISBN:
　　　　Softcover: 978-1-961210-02-8

　　　　eBook: 978-1-961210-03-5

All rights reserved. No part of this book may be reproduced or transmitted in any form or by any means, electronic or mechanical, including photocopying, recording, or by any information storage and retrieval system, without permission in writing from the copyright owner.

This is a work of fiction. Names, characters, places and incidents either are the product of the author's imagination or are used fictitiously, and any resemblance to any actual persons, living or dead, events, or locales is entirely coincidental.

Any people depicted in stock imagery provided by Getty Images are models, and such images are being used for illustrative purposes only. Certain stock imagery © Getty Images.

Print information available on the last page.

Rev. date:

To order additional copies of this book, contact:

Contents

Dedication		v
Acknowledgments		vii
1. Greetings and Salutations		1
2. Well, That's One Way to Start a Day		9
3. Art Gallery		17
4. Dorks, Spirits, and Bears…Oh, My!		23
5. Well…Hello, There, Handsome		31
6. You Probably Shouldn't Have Said That		37
7. I Picked These Just for You		43
8. Death by Bouquet		51
9. Today's Sermon		59
10. Youthful Indiscretions		67
11. Freudian and Other Unfortunate Slips		75
12. The Foreplay is Now Over		83
13. Wrong on Multiple Levels		91
14. The Fury of Redemption…or is That Furry?		99
15. Blood is an Acquired Taste		107
16. Seriously, How Many Family Secrets Do We Need?		113
17. The Pitfalls of Peer Pressure		119
18. Dead Beat Dads		127
19. Aloha		139
20. Queen High Flush		147
21. Hey! You Didn't RSVP!		157
22. Woo Girls and Nuptials		169
23. Sister Act		179

Dedication

This book is dedicated to my beautiful, strong, and intelligent wife, Pam. Without your support, I would never have been able to create this work. I thank you, and I love you. These books literally and figuratively represent a new chapter in our adventure together, and there's no one else on this earth that I would want to be on this ride with.

This book is also dedicated to every person who has suffered a loss at the hands of the sadistic bullies in our world.

It is dedicated to our Asian brothers and sisters who suffer from harassment.

It is dedicated to our Hispanic brothers and sisters who are looked down upon by large segments of our society.

It is dedicated to our Native American brothers and sisters who continue to suffer under the yoke of American colonialism.

It is dedicated to our sisters who are losing their rights of self-determination in their personal health care.

It is dedicated to our veterans who have yet to have a national healthcare system worthy of their sacrifice.

It is dedicated to every person who lost someone to COVID-19 because the lemmings around them weren't taking this shit seriously.

It is dedicated to every person, especially children, who must carry the scars of mental, physical, and sexual abuse.

It is dedicated to every person who has lost a loved one because of the senseless proliferation of guns in our society.

It is dedicated to every one of our Black brothers and sisters who has lost a loved one by execution on our streets at the hands of our broken criminal justice system.

It is dedicated to every LGBTQ+ person who continues to be discriminated against, targeted, and marginalized.

It is dedicated to every woman who has to endure the leering glances and unwelcome advances of their male counterparts.

And finally, it is dedicated to every person whose voting rights and voice in our democracy have been compromised because of bullshit, tinfoil-hat conspiracy theories.

I weep with you. I scream with you. I stand with you. And I love you all.

Acknowledgments

I would like to thank so many people whose aggregated influences and inspiration have culminated in the creation of this work.

I thank my parents, Mike and Carla, for instilling in me basic ethics and morality. I miss you, Dad, and it is my prayer that this work puts a smile on your angelic face.

I thank my sister, Paige, for her creativity and decency.

I thank my sister, Cory, for her boundless optimism and wisdom.

I thank my niece, Hannah, for being one of the strongest people I have ever known.

I thank my niece, Faye, for her originality and humanity.

I thank my nephew, Thomas and my niece, Brin, for being the inspiration behind many of my characters' childlike qualities and for always making me smile.

I thank my in-laws, for their welcoming love, cookies, and beef and noodles.

I thank Todd for his friendship and endless patience with me.

I thank Amy for her steadiness and friendship.

I thank Kara for her irreverent personality and feedback on my work.

I thank Marcia for her kind and gentle soul.

I thank Wes and all my friends from Pallister's for making me laugh and being my oasis of sanity.

I thank Michael, Mike, Peter, and Bill, for providing a large piece of my life's personal soundtrack. Please come back to us. We need you now more than ever.

I thank Bruce Springsteen for teaching me how emotionally moving art can be.

I thank Lux Interior, for his over-the-top attitude and punk rock inspiration. Thank you for showing me that artists can do things their own way and not compromise their vision. That art can sometimes be beautifully messy and non-conformist. Rest in peace, my friend.

I thank Joe Bob Briggs for introducing me to horrific wonders in his most unique manner.

And finally, and perhaps somewhat surprisingly, I would like to thank all of the pricks who have belittled me, lied to me, lied about me, and stabbed me in the back throughout my life. You are the inspiration behind my "fuck off" attitude. You inspired me to create these characters. So, thank you for being the assholes that you have always been and will always be. Time's up, bitches! Evan out!

Chapter 1

Greetings and Salutations

The grandfather clock chimed at exactly midnight to usher in September 1, 2034. At that moment, she was awoken with a start. Her tie-dyed T-shirt and red plaid boxer shorts were saturated with her own sweat. Her pupils expanded to allow what little light that there was into her deep hazel eyes. Her eyes continued expanding as a dark purple cloud formed at the foot of her bed. The eerie cloud continued its transformation into the loose form of a lanky female with glowing red eyes and what appeared to be a tight bun of copper hair upon its misty head. Her eyes widened as the gaseous form began a high-pitched cackle that sent shivers down her spine. She pinched herself. It was just a dream.

At that moment, she was awoken with a start. Her tie-dyed T-shirt and red plaid boxer shorts were saturated with her own sweat. Her pupils expanded to allow what little light that there was into her deep hazel eyes. Her eyes continued expanding as a dark purple cloud formed at the foot of her bed. The eerie cloud continued its transformation into the loose form of a lanky female with glowing red eyes and what appeared to be a tight bun of copper hair upon its misty head. Her eyes widened as the gaseous form began a high-pitched cackle that sent shivers down her spine. She pinched herself. It was just a dream.

At that moment, she was awoken with a start. Her tie-dyed T-shirt and red plaid boxer shorts were saturated with her own sweat. Her pupils expanded to allow what little light that there was into her deep hazel eyes. Her eyes continued expanding as a dark purple cloud formed at the foot of her bed. The eerie cloud continued its transformation into the loose form of a lanky female with glowing red eyes and what appeared to be a tight bun of copper hair upon its misty head. Her eyes widened as the gaseous form began a high-pitched cackle that sent shivers down her spine. She pinched herself. "Ow!" she exclaimed. This was not a dream.

The unearthly dark purple form continued its cackling as it floated slowly upon her bed. It continued its effortless path, leaving a pungent trail of sticky, purple residue upon the young woman's body. It peered down at her with her emblazoned crimson eyes and ceased its cackling. It frowned at the frozen young woman and screamed in a high-pitched, nasally voice, "Stay away from her! Stay out of this! She is mine! You will *not* be warned again!"

At that moment, she was awoken with a start. Her tie-dyed T-shirt and red plaid boxer shorts were saturated with her own sweat. Her entire body had a purple molasses-like residue on it. Her boxer shorts were soaked from having wet herself. She was trembling. She vigorously shook her head to shake the nightmarish encounter from her consciousness, went to the bathroom and looked at her bloodshot eyes in the mirror. *What the hell did they put in that stuff last night?* she wondered to herself as she was finally coming to grips that this experience had been nothing more than a really bad trip. And that the previous night's party must have been much messier than what she remembered.

"Eeeewwww"! she cried out as the hot water rinsed the purple slime from her five-foot seven full figured caramel skinned body. She scrubbed intensely in order to wash the ooze from her tight Rastafarian shoulder length braids.

She made her way down the rickety stairs of the three-bedroom New Orleans home that she shared with her three best friends. "Well good morning sweetheart! What is up with all the screaming?" Jamie Johnson beamed as she made her way into the living room and handed the still slightly trembling Arima Azan a steaming cup of jet-black coffee. Jamie's floral nightgown rode up to briefly expose her despised member as she sat on the couch next to her best friend since kindergarten. "Oopsie!" she declared through her laughter. "Better put *that* one away. *That* is *not* for you.

And, hopefully not for *me* soon. So....tell me...what was with the screaming?"

Arima looked at her coffee with disinterest and said, "Ah, its nothin'. Just a bad trip, I guess. But it seemed so real. I don't even want to talk about it. It still creeps me out. I just need to lay off the weed for today. Y'know, get my system cleaned out or somethin'. Nope, *not* gonna smoke at all today".

Jamie looked at her best friend with a wide-eyed and bemused expression as she continued to listen to Arima. "Nope, none for me today, thanks. Well...at least not before dinner. I need to maybe just make that a nighttime activity or something. Or...well...*definitely* not before lunch. I already pig out enough *without* a case of the munchies. Save it up for the early afternoon, that's my new motto." Arima surveyed the coffee table that was littered with pizza boxes, beer cans, mail, magazines, and a *lot* of stems. Noticing the objects that she was looking for, she hazily said, "Hey...hand me that pipe and baggie wouldja? But I'm *definitely* gonna start that other thing tomorrow. Or maybe the next day. Well...we'll just see how it goes."

"What is going on?" came the desperate cry of a woman's voice from the downstairs bedroom. "Uh...I dunno baby, I'm really trying" came a male's response. "Well...try putting it in there!" the woman demanded. "You know that I already tried that! It doesn't fit there!" the man roared back.

Arima and Jamie stared at each other in shocked silence with gleeful smiles upon their faces as they continued to listen to this uncharacteristic marital squabble between Jessie and Cliff West. "C'mon baby," Jessie pleaded. "You *know* I need it first thing in the morning. Make it work!" "I'm telling you I'm trying but...its just dead. Its just lying there. Nothing is working! I can't get it up!" came the exasperated reply of her beloved husband Cliff. "Fine! I'll just use Jamie's then!"

The petite, pink camisole-clad blonde figure came into the living room with determination and stood in front of her bewildered trans friend. "Give it to me," Jessie demanded. "Um...um...um....give *what* to you?" came Jamie's hesitant inquiry. The impatient Jessie replied, "Your phone. Neither of ours is working and you know how I have to check my likes every morning. Give it to me. Where is it?"

"Oh...*that*...alrighty then, sweetie. *That* I can give to you. I'll just get it from my bedroom," a relieved Jamie responded as she wiped sweat from her brow.

"What's wrong with her?" Jessie asked Arima as Jamie ascended the staircase towards her bedroom.

"Um...well," Arima began as she attempted to think of how to put this delicately. "We weren't quite sure what you guys were doing and...well...it kinda sounded like you wanted to use Jamie's dick."

Jessie burst out in hysterical laughter as her husband entered the room, still in his pajamas. "She thought *what*? That I wanted to use her *dick*? I mean...I've *always* fantasized about maybe having an interracial thing with a Black dude, but if that happens, I'd prefer that I'm with somebody who is actually into me, y'know?"

"Wait...what?" a confused Cliff asked as his wife playfully patted his ass, looked up at him with a grin and said, "Don't worry, baby. It's just a fantasy. You are quite...adequate."

"Yeah, that's reassuring," Cliff replied as he made his way to the kitchen. "Do you want some eggs?"

"Sure, baby! Right after I feast on all of my likes!" Jessie hungrily replied as she grabbed the iPhone from Jamie's hand.

"What...the...*hell*?" Jessie screamed out once again. "I know that I paid the Internet. It comes right out of my account. Turn on the TV. Let's see if something's going on."

Arima dug into the couch cushions, found the remote mingled with lint and stale corn chips, and pressed the power button. The TV came on, but none of the streaming services were operational.

"This is *really* starting to piss me off!" Jessie roared as she flipped open her laptop and began searching the web for information. The computer would not connect. Jessie sat silently as tears began to form in her eyes. "Hey, baby?" she meekly stated to her husband. "Could you just hold me? Something's wrong. I can't get to my feeds. I can't post anything. I can't see my likes and my loves. I'm...I'm...lost."

Arima looked at her friend with no expression and stated flatly, "Y'know, maybe this is a good thing. You're becoming addicted to that shit."

"Addicted?" Jessie roared back. "Oh, that's *really* rich coming from the stoner of the year! Year? Hell, stoner of the *decade*! I'm *not* addicted. But I have followers who hang on my *every word*. My every action. My every experience. They are *lost* without my guidance. What I do is provide advice and funny memes to help people through their day! Now, what are *they* going to do?"

"Um...I dunno," Arima replied. "Probably just find some other way to blow off their jobs and waste their time. Well, good luck with that. I've gotta get dressed and go over to Gram's. Then I've gotta go to that job interview at the morgue."

"And then, sweetie," Jamie gushed. "You will be meeting *us* for your twenty-third birthday celebration!"

"Oh yeah," Arima replied whimsically. "It's my birthday. I guess I forgot what day it was. Looking forward to the birthday brownies."

As Arima began up the stairs, she heard Jessie exclaim once again as she broke down into tears, "Why won't this *work*? What is going *on*? This is the worst thing that has *ever happened*!"

Jamie found and turned on a small radio. Out of the tiny speaker came static, then an announcer's voice declaring, *"Once again, all wireless internet services throughout the world have been compromised and taken offline. Repair crews are baffled as to the cause of the constant power overloads and are unable to restore the service for any period of time greater than five minutes. As of right now, it appears that the only way that internet service can be accessed is through outdated phone lines and landline modems. We will keep you updated as this tragic event unfolds. This emergency news break has been brought to you by NoSkids laundry detergent. Leave your mark by leaving NoSkids today!"*

"Oh...my....GAAAAAAWD!" Jessie wailed out as she flew out of the room and flung herself face-first onto her bed crying hysterically. "Well, shit," Jamie stated as she slowly shook her head. "There goes my internet porn". Cliff just looked at the floor and silently nodded.

―――

Arima was nearly bowled over by the seven young school-children as they were hastily leaving her grandmother's house to begin their first day of school. Louise Azan's sixty-two-year-old tan face beamed with pride as she watched her well-fed neighbor children scurry down the block.

She then looked at the beautiful young woman standing in her doorway. Arima was her pride and joy. She had raised her since birth following the tragic loss of her daughter shortly after her granddaughter's emergence into the world. She chuckled to herself as she remembered holding her newly born granddaughter for the first time twenty-three years ago. She was then, as she was now. Mellow. Arima very rarely made a sound as an infant with the exception of some light cooing. Her caramel skin was the product of her all-Jamaican mother and western European... Her mind forced the thought of Arima's biological father out of her head. He was not worth even a second of consideration. She focused instead once again on her beautiful granddaughter.

As a child, Arima loved everybody and everything. She was a pure soul who was always eager to help others in need, although she would do so at her own pace and in her own time. Nothing was ever urgent to her, but when something important needed to be done, she possessed the quick intellect and ability to apply herself in order to complete the task at hand. Usually without too much grumbling. She adored nature, especially animals, and took it upon herself to shelter and feed as many neighborhood strays as she could.

As a teenager, she began volunteering at a local animal shelter. Upon graduation from high school- which was finally completed as her taskmaster grandmother stood over her shoulder to ensure that she completed all of her missed assignments- she became a full-time employee at the shelter.

She moved out of her house and moved in with her lifelong friends at the age of twenty-one. Louise was aware of the parties and of Arima's other more pungent interests. She was not at all surprised when Arima began smoking in her late teens. In fact, although Louise did not imbibe in this herself at this stage of her life, she tacitly approved of Arima's participation as long as it did not interfere with her being able to support herself.

There was really no difference between that and casual consumption of alcohol, she thought. And, this form of escape was much more in keeping with her nonchalant and low-key persona. Alcohol, Louise believed, was responsible for summoning the demons that reside in each of us. Marijuana served to keep them away.

At least this is what Louise hoped was the case as she continued to gaze upon her granddaughter on this, her fateful twenty-third birthday. It was on this day that every female Azan descendent had learned about the full extent of their special gift to the world. The type of energy that they possessed would reveal itself in its true form and the honing of that power would begin under the tutelage of her female elders. Louise felt that she knew what her beloved granddaughter's special feminine ability would be. It would be to communicate with the spirit world and to guide them onto the realm of Enlightenment where their souls could watch over and guide others who remained upon the earth.

She smiled and cupped Arima's cheeks in her hands. She gazed deeply into her granddaughter's hazel eyes. Her smile faded and she began trembling. Her beautiful granddaughter could indeed guide hapless spirits into Enlightenment. Tears formed in her eyes as she now realized that her granddaughter could also be used, inhabited by, and manipulated by the more maniacal spirits in this universe. The soulless. The demons. Louise could feel it in her very essence. It was one of *her* gifts. It would take more than a few tokes off of a joint to keep these demons away. It would take concerted effort and training to give her trusting granddaughter the tools that she needed in order to remain a pure soul. And it would require that she have the conversation with her beloved granddaughter that she had longed dreaded and prayed would never be necessary. She had to tell Arima the story of her father.

Chapter 2

Well, That's One Way to Start a Day

"Come inside this instant, my child," Louise stated with urgency as Arima replied, "Sure. What's the rush, Grams?"

"Oh, my child, sit with me. We need to have a talk." As Arima sat next to her grandmother on her floral couch in the main sitting room, she looked around at the walls which were adorned with paintings and sculptures from their native Jamaica. Arima had always been comforted by being surrounded by her heritage in this room. But today was different. As she looked upon the colorful artifacts today, she saw things in them that she had not noticed before. She saw things that were unsettling. Dark shadows and silhouettes swirled throughout the artwork that had not been there before. She thought about the urgency of her grandmother's demeanor, and she shuddered.

"Um...so what's up Grams? What's with all of the drama?"

"Give me your hands, child, and look into my eyes," came Louise's cordial demand. "Look deeply into my eyes, my lovely. Now...tell me what you saw last night."

"Uh...last night? Nothing really. Just a weird nightmare. I gotta stop getting my stuff from that guy. His quality control is really going downhill," came Arima's nonchalant reply.

"Tell me about it, child. Tell me about who you saw," Louise replied impatiently.

"Uh...I don't know. It was just, like, this weird purple ghost crazy bitch. She had red eyes and told me to stay out of something. That she was hers. I haven't a clue what it means. She was large and purple, so maybe just a weird Freudian penis envy thing in my subconscious. Plus, I had some weird purple yuck on me after the dream, so...yep...probably penis envy."

"She left a residue," Louise inquired hesitantly.

"Uh...no...it wasn't the *dream*," Arima replied through her light chuckles. "I musta just spilled something on myself. It was just a dream, Grams. Nothin' to get uptight about. I know you have your rituals and beliefs but I...well...I respect them, but I don't really believe in that stuff."

"Tell me, child, *exactly* what this apparition looked like," Louise demanded.

"Ummmm...I don't know. Like I said, just a weird purple mist or something. Tall, lanky, glowing red eyes. Y'know...the standard nightmare ghost stuff. Oh...this was a bit strange though. She had a tight bun of copper hair on her head. Kind of a weird detail in a dream, dontcha think?"

Louise began trembling. Her mind was immediately transported back to an evening three weeks prior when she was sitting and watching one of her stories on television. The screen had gone black just before the final reveal of who the killer was. Disgusted, Louise turned the TV off, then on again. Instead of the program, a dark purple static emerged from the screen, casting the entire room in its eerie regal glow. A pair of glowing red eyes appeared and a diabolically misty form began to emerge from the television. It was nine feet tall and impossibly lanky. It had a tight bun of copper hair upon its head, and it spoke in an evil, nasally voice.

"Your granddaughter is quite beautiful," the wicked specter began. "Yes, quite beautiful, indeed. And soon she will be quite gifted. She will be called to assist one of my own. She will be called to interfere. This *must* not happen. I am warning you now just as I will warn her upon her twenty-third birthday when *she* will be able to hear me. If she interferes with me, I will *destroy* her. I will destroy *you*. I will *destroy* everything that you both hold dear. She will listen to you. Tell her to never go to New York. *Ever*. Tell her to stay away. It is *not* her fight. Tell her..."

The floating grotesque figure bent down to look Louise directly into her fear-stricken eyes and concluded in a demonic growl, "Tell her or I will rip her from her insides out and hang her from the highest tree. Tell her or the ravens will feast upon her intestines as she desperately clings to life. Tell her or she *will die* a most gruesome death. *TELL HER!*" At that moment, the apparition dissipated and the television came back on. Louise just sat there trembling in shock.

Louise stared once again at her beloved granddaughter before getting up and taking a picture off of the mantle. She placed the photograph of a beautiful woman of Jamaican descent into Arima's hands. Arima gazed at the picture of the full-figured beauty, her smile beaming and her face glowing with happiness. She was holding her newborn child.

"Uh, yeah?" the perplexed Arima began. "So…why did you hand me this picture of my mother?"

"My dearest," Louise began with trepidation. "This picture was taken on the day your mother brought you home. This was your third day in this world and your mother was so happy. She was so proud. And she was so relieved. Relieved that your father was finally out of her life. The divorce proceedings were concluded just a few days prior to your birth. He signed away custody of you. And your mother was…free.

"I know that we have never spoken about your father, but we must do so today. You must understand who he truly was so that you may understand who you truly have become on this day. You must listen to me, my darling. You must *listen*. You must *understand*. And you must *accept* my guidance. Do you understand?"

"Uh…I guess so," Arima replied as she began feeling increasingly uncomfortable with her grandmother's demeanor and the path that the discussion was taking.

"I never wanted to discuss your father with you, but I knew that the day would come when I was forced to do so. Today is that day. Your father had been a pastor but became a traveling salesman. He was quite good at what he did. He was so charming. So charismatic. So handsome…except for his disfigured hands." Louise's voice then dropped as she continued. "So manipulative. So overbearing. So controlling. So sadistic. So evil. He was the con man's con man. He could sell Satan to the missionaries. And he did.

"He was a soldier for the demon Vetis, the Tempter of the Holy. He was one of many throughout the world who would lie to and manipulate the weak-minded. He would manipulate them into turning their backs on their holy beliefs, whether they be Christian, Jew, Muslim, Buddhist or any of the other great religious philosophies. He would manipulate them into believing that they had a God-given dominion over this earth. He would manipulate them into hating all of those that did not follow him. He would manipulate them into committing heinous acts of violence and bloodshed in his name.

"It was all in preparation for the arrival of Vetis. We have seen this play out over the last two decades in our country and all over the world. Horrendous populace uprisings that have attempted to overthrow our world's great democracies and replace them with tyrannical dictatorships. It was thought by many that the orange one was the embodiment of Vetis when he rose to power in 2016. He was not. He was just another hapless pawn put in place to continue to move the needle towards hell on earth. And that period was just another scene in a very long movie. A movie that has yet to play out. And one of your father's orders was to place someone upon this earth that could fight alongside him when Vetis made his final push for world domination. Someone with special abilities. That is why he sought out your mother. He knew that your mother would soon possess *her* special abilities and could give birth to his unholy seed. He seduced her, impregnated her and dominated her. But he miscalculated the strength of the Azar womanhood. We fought back. *She* fought back. And like all petty little bullies, he slinked back into his swamp at the first sign of fortitude. Although things seem to be stabilizing around the world at the moment, this is but the calm before the storm. And your father and all of the millions of knowing soldiers and unwitting followers of Vetis are continuing to prepare for the final battle. I do not know when this battle will be waged, but I know that you are a key part of your father's plans. I know that he will return for you. That is why I have nurtured and protected you. And I shall do so always, even beyond my parting breath."

"Okay. Grams?" Arima replied without knowing how exactly to respond. "Um...listen. Maybe we need to go see your doctor, huh? Maybe one of your heart pills is messing you up a little. Do you want me to maybe make an appointment? Besides, if Mom was away from this jerk and was so happy, then why did she run away? Why did she abandon me? I'm sorry, Grams, but this all seems a bit...far-fetched. And that's coming from someone who is *really* buzzed right now."

Louise looked up at the ceiling with a bemused expression on her face. With a tone of resolve she said as she continued to look upward, "Yes, I must tell her now. You are correct, my dear. She must know...everything."

"Ummm...Grams? Who are ya talkin' to?" a confused Arima inquired as she was beginning to think that she may need to reschedule her job interview at the city morgue in order to take her beloved grandmother to an appointment for a *different* kind of doctor.

"Yes, my darling," Louise began again as her gaze fell upon her granddaughter's perplexed face. "You were told that your mother abandoned you. That she was a free spirit who simply could not be tied down. That was the story. And that was a lie. And I am sorry that I had you believe that for all of these years. Look again at your mother's picture, my dear. Look deeply. Focus on the love that I know that you have for her. What do you see?"

Arima let out a deep sigh of disregard, rolled her eyes, and stared at the picture. She experienced her conflicted feelings of love and disdain for the woman who had given birth to her, then abandoned her three days later. She felt tears begin to well up in her slightly bloodshot eyes as her feelings began to overwhelm her psyche. And then, she saw it. Her mother's image began glowing and her smile began to widen. The woman in the picture gave her daughter a playful wink of her eye. And her daughter sat there transfixed on the beauty of her mother and her mother's love that she now could feel penetrate her soul.

"Wha...wha...what is happening?" is all that Arima could manage before her grandmother began once again.

"Listen to me. Your mother did not abandon you. A few hours after this picture was taken, your father called one final time. He told her that although he would not be involved with you, he still wanted to make arrangements for your future. Just one final meeting and then he would be out of her life forever. I pleaded with her not to go, but her youthful nineteen-year-old mind did not heed my warnings. Despite all of the treachery at that man's hands, he never was able to beat her carefree spirit and optimism out of her. Perhaps it should have been. She did not return that evening. She did not *ever* return. She was found three days later on an altar in the swamp. She had been cut open and her insides were splayed all over the dark grey granite. Her head was on a pike. And that was the last image that I ever had of your mother. My daughter. My lovely Abdalla."

Louise began a slight nervous chuckle as she lit a candle on top of the mantle. "He should have known. He should have seen that she would never completely submit to him. But I suppose he wanted a challenge. And he was assured that their offspring would be quite powerful. But still, he should have known. You see, 'Abdalla' means 'servant of God'.

"Um...um...um," was Arima's response as her mind began trying to wrap itself around what she had just been told. *What? My mother was to have special powers that she could pass on to me? So that I could fight at my sadistic father's side? My father who murdered my mother? So that some weird dick of a demon could take over the world? And now I'm seeing weird forms in the artwork and my mother's picture is winking at me? And to top it off...that creepy bitch last night was real? Oh man, this is too much. I need a hit.*

"Oh, my darling Arima," Louise began again in an understanding tone. "I know this is a lot to take in. And smoking dope is *not* going to help you process this right now. There are forces who have been waiting for you to come of age. And that has happened on this day. I had always hoped that it would only be the forces of the righteous who would be able to employ your special abilities. But I'm sorry to say, my dear, that you are a product of both your mother *and* your father. Your special ability is to be able to sense when spirits are trapped here. Spirits who have more work to do before they can move on to Enlightenment so that they may watch over and guide their earthbound loved ones. You will be able to sense them, let them into your soul, and assist them in completing their earthly work so that they may then move on.

"And if you are able to find another woman with special abilities, a woman who can harness and discharge spiritual energy, then it may be possible for the two of you to place that spirit into another living being. You have the ability to make the connection and bring it into our realm and into your soul. The other would be able to capture that spirit's energy and place it into another's body. Then, that spirit will be able to complete their work on this earth in a new human form.

"But there is a troubling side to your gift. A dangerous side. An evil side. If you are not careful, a maniacal spirit may be able to possess your soul and use you for their treacherous will. That is what your father has planned for you. And the evil spirit that came to you last night may possess that ability. She perhaps is a demonic force that is acting in concert with your father. She is very strong. I know. I, too, have been visited by her. I, too, was warned by her. I am pleading with you Arima. Take her warnings seriously. Whatever it is that she is involved in, it is not your battle. I do not know when, but it appears that at some point in your life you will be summoned to New York. *Do not go!* Ignore it. Live your life and *do not* be manipulated into someone else's battles. And I do not know why, but I find it very strange that all of this has happened on the day that the wireless internet has been knocked out by some unexplained force. I just get the feeling that that force may be the source of trouble for you. Heed that devil's warning, Arima. Heed *my* warning. If you do nothing else for me in your life, promise me this one thing: do *not* go to New York. Ever."

Chapter 3

Art Gallery

"Not planning on it...especially now," came Arima's uninterested response. "So, anyway Grams, you got any tea made? My throats kinda dry from... well, heh, heh...you know."

"Of course, darling," Louise replied thoughtfully as she gave her beloved granddaughter a light kiss upon her tan forehead. "And perhaps some of my sugar cookies?"

"Yeah, that would be good," Arima replied. "I need something to help me calm my nerves. You just laid a ton on me, Grams, and...I mean...maybe my eyes are playing tricks on me. I could have sworn I saw my mother's picture wink at me. I dunno. This is pretty messed up, Grams."

"I know it is my dearest," Louise replied softly as she began making her way toward the kitchen. Louise was out of Arima's earshot when she concluded her thought with, "This is indeed quite messed up. And this, I fear, is just the calm before the storm."

Arima stared at her mother's picture. She picked it up and moved it to the left, to the right, and tipped it at every angle so as to try to recreate the shadow and light pattern that had created the earlier hallucination. The picture's image never changed. It remained a static photograph of her mother's angelic, smiling face.

Okay, okay. Just another weird experience left over from that batch of dope. Nothin' to be concerned about Arima thought to herself as her anxiety began to subside. She began laughing out loud at the absurdity of what her grandmother had just told her. *Oh, Grams! You have always been good at practical jokes, but this one takes the cake! And on my birthday, no less. I wonder how long this crazy ol' broad has been cooking this up. Yep, nothing more than one of her jokes like she used to play with me as a child to get me up in the mornings or to get me to do my homework. She just wants me on edge so that I take this interview seriously. And I really do need this job since the animal shelter moved to its new location. All right, Grams, I guess I'll just play along and not disappoint you today.*

Arima then burst into laughter as she thought about the previous jokes that her grandmother had played on her throughout her life. Her poorly attempted homework that would mysteriously disappear so that she would have to do it all over again. But correctly this time. Turning the heat down in the winter and whipping her blankets off of her in order to force her to get up and start a new day. Replacing her junk food stash of candy and chips with fruit and granola bars. The list of jokes was endless. But they did serve to give Arima the required nudge in the right direction to keep her motivated and keep her proceeding through her life. And Arima never gave her grandmother the satisfaction of acknowledging her little pranks. She simply accepted the lesson and never mentioned it to her. *Nope, never gave her the satisfaction,* Arima thought to herself as she wiped amused tears from her eyes while continuing her laughter and looking up at a painting.

It was one of her favorites. A beautiful scene of the sun setting over a Jamaican harbor, the brilliant oranges and yellows being reflected off of the lush green of the palm trees and brilliant blue of the lapping waves. This painting had always calmed her as a child as she allowed her mind to bask in the warm glow of her motherland. This painting had always called to her.

As she stared at the artwork, it gradually became darker. Black clouds began to form which blotted out the brilliance of the setting sun. The grand leaves on the majestic palms began to dry and wither. The enchanting blue waves turned dark red.

Arima stared in disbelief and immediately ceased her laughter once a pair of dark grey eyes emerged at the top of the painting, and it began cackling. *What the hell are you laughing at, bitch?* the newly formed mouth stated as an evil-looking face began protruding beyond the wooden frame of the canvas. *I have been stuck in this damned picture for centuries! I've been waiting for you! Waiting for the time that you will be able to help me! And you will help me or else I will...*

Arima let out a ghastly shriek as Louise entered the room with the tea and cookies. The twisted face immediately receded and the painting returned to its initial beauty. Arima looked at her bemused grandmother and stammered, "The painting...in the painting...there was a face...a *horrible* face demanding that I help him...what the *hell*, Grams? What the hell is *happening* to me? This isn't one of your practical jokes, is it? This shit is really *happening*!"

Louise set the tray of tea and cookies upon the worn coffee table as she chuckled and shook her head. "Oh, I see that you've met Howard. I was wondering when he might try to connect with you," she said to Arima's fearfully bewildered face.

"Who...the hell...is *Howard*?" Arima screamed out.

"Well, dear," Louise began calmly as she poured the tea into a flowered porcelain cup. "Howard was a dreadful man. He controlled the importing and exporting of African slaves through Jamaica to his homeland of Virginia. He was especially brutal, even for those times. His retribution against even the slightest of infractions was swift and merciless. The removal of tongues. Vicious beatings. Even more vicious rapes of the poor slave women. He was a monster. But he had a vulnerability."

"He absolutely adored the darker complexion and beauty of Jamaican women. To say that he was a womanizer would be quite an understatement indeed. And, although impossibly brutal, he always longed for a beautiful Jamaican woman that he could wed and bring home with him. Now this was, of course, not only taboo but illegal at that time, so he met a woman and fell under her intoxicating spell. Following a short courtship, he wed her secretly in Jamaica and brought her to his plantation in Virginia under the guise of being his house servant. He truly did love her, I do believe.

"And I also believe that his bride loved murdering him at the first chance that she had upon her arrival in her new home. This woman had two things that she wanted to accomplish. The first was that she desired safe passage to the newly formed United States without fear of becoming enslaved herself. The second was that she wanted revenge against this vile man that she had witnessed committing the most abhorrent atrocities to other human beings.

"So, in 1789, three days after her twenty-third birthday, she wed Howard and was immediately brought to Virginia with him. As the story goes, they consummated their marriage that night as her impatient eyes gazed upon this very painting that she had brought with her. As he achieved…well…as he was finishing his business which would result in a daughter, she took a dagger from underneath her pillow and plunged it into the man's neck. It is said that no one in the house thought much of his shrieking as he was always quite loud when he was involved in such activities.

"As he lay there dying, she made connection with his…well…not his *soul*. Men like that do not have a *soul* to speak of. She made connection with his essence, drew it out of his body, and banished it into this painting for all of eternity. Since that fateful evening, Howard's essence has been trapped there, burning in the constantly setting sun and drowning in the cool water simultaneously. I suppose that he has had quite an unpleasant time of it. And deservingly so. And, if he has frightened you and is being demanding of you, then I am guessing…"

Louise's voice trailed off as she looked up at the painting and smirked. "I am guessing, Howard, that despite the years upon years that you have been trapped in there that you have not *learned* your *lesson*. I am guessing that you are *still* the same miserable son of a bitch as that night my namesake placed you in there. Have you learned nothing? Are you still the same brutally racist and sexist deplorable that you had always been? You can try to frighten Arima all you like. But you *need to learn* that she will *not* respond to your silly little threats or intimidation. *You need to learn* that you will catch many more flies with honey than vinegar. You need to learn that or there will be *nobody* to *ever* assist you in releasing you so that you may ascend to Enlightenment. Now…you just *sit* in that painting and *think about that* as you watch yet *another* generation slip out of your grasp. So there!"

"Wait, Grams," Arima inquired in the most animated cadence that she had ever uttered. "Your namesake? You said that this Jamaican woman was your namesake. Who was she? What happened to her?"

"She, my lovely, was the very first Louise Azan," Louise replied wistfully. "She left that house under the cover of night that very evening and went on a journey that finally ended in the land that would become Louisiana. She is your…let's see now…how many would there be? Ah, yes. She would be your great, great, great, great, great, great grandmother. She was the original Azan to live in this land. And she began the tradition of quite powerful and gifted Azan women. My mother saw *my* special gifts upon my birth and named me after her, which I have *always* considered to be the greatest of family honors.

"Although I never cared much for my family nickname. You see dear, that is why everyone in my family calls me 'Junior.' Because I am the second 'Louise' in this family. I have also been referred to as 'LJ' or 'Louise, Junior.' I suppose it doesn't matter much, but it did provide fuel for when I felt like placing snakes in my brother's bed, heh, heh, heh. He was such a nice boy, but so very gullible. I wish that you had been able to meet him. But he was taken from us at a young age. My destiny was to raise you, I have since learned. His destiny was to go to Enlightenment and watch over me. To guide me. To protect me from there. And he has. Every morning, I go to my window and say hello to his spirit. Then, the little chirping bird containing my brother's spirit will fly away, content that his sister still remembers and adores him. But that is a story for another time."

"So," Arima responded as her mind whirled through a slight veil of THC and a thick veil of confusion. "So this is all *real*? Everything that you have told me? About my *mother*? My *father*? A *demon* wanting to rise to power over the earth by lying to and manipulating those that profess to be holy? None of this is one of your practical jokes?"

"Everything that I have told you is real, my darling," Louise responded sincerely. "But I do not know what you mean by my practical jokes. What are you referring to, dear?"

"Oh! C'mon, Grams!" Arima exclaimed. "You know how you would hide my homework so that I would have to do it over. Or when you would replace my snacks with fruit and stuff. Or pull my blankets off of me so that I'd get cold and wake up in the morning. Listen, I never wanted to give you the satisfaction of knowing your little pranks worked, so I never talked to you about it. And it was a pretty clever way to get me going sometimes. But you can drop the ruse. Just admit that you used to pull those pranks on me. I believe everything that you've just told me, but just come clean on the pranks."

Louise burst out into a deep, guttural, booming laugh that bounced around the room and echoed off the artistically adorned walls. She finally gained her composure and wiped a joyful tear from her eye. She placed her hands upon the cheeks of her beloved granddaughter, stared into her brown eyes and said gleefully, "Oh, my darling. That wasn't *me*. That was your *mother*."

"Sure, sure. Of course it was," Arima replied with subdued resignation. "Yup. My dead mother's spirit played pranks on me. Sure. Makes perfect sense. Well, Grams, I think this is just about as much family time as I can deal with at the moment. I think I'll just head out to my interview and see how strange *that* gets. Then my birthday party. Yep. It's been a banner day".

"And your interview is at the morgue, dear?" Louise inquired.

"Yeah, it's just like an overnight security kind of a gig. All I have to do is watch over the stiffs and fill out some paperwork if a new one comes in. Should be just a lot of sitting around and playing on my phone. Should give me lots of time to send snarky replies to Jessie's self-absorbed posts, heh, heh, heh. I mean, if that's even a thing again. Wow, what a weird day".

"My lovely," Louise stated as the pair got up from their seats. "If you get a job at the morgue, I have a feeling that you may not have much time for playing on your silly little contraption. I have a feeling that there are a number of Howards out there that may vie for your attention. I have a feeling that this may be quite an interesting experience for you. But if you take this job, and you are contacted by souls who are unable to move on to Enlightenment, you must tell me about them before you allow them in. And if you are ever visited again by that copper-headed monstrosity...well...just tell me and do exactly as she says. I do not get frightened easily. I have seen many things in my sixty-two years. But I have never been in the presence of such evil in my life. So, please, darling. Be careful, all right?"

"Of course, Grams," Arima replied as she gave her grandmother a loving embrace.

As Arima and Louise departed the living room and began walking toward the front door, a painting on the opposite wall of Howard's began giggling. Howard's black eyes peered across the room at the three swirling dark silhouettes in the painting and said sinisterly, *You three leave her alone. She is mine!*

Chapter 4

Dorks, Spirits, and Bears...
Oh, My!

Jeez, this place is creepy. Could it kill them to put up a couple pictures? Arima thought to herself as she stared at the grey concrete walls in the office of the morgue's manager. She sat there nervously shuffling her feet, causing her brightly-colored flowered dress to sway slightly. She felt beads of sweat begin to form on her forehead as she watched this middle-aged Caucasian man with a very bad comb over and thick glasses carefully review her resume.

"So," the man began in a dry, uninterested tone, "It seems as though you have no experience in this field then?"

"Uh, no, uh…Mr. Man…um…Manfren…um…," Arima stammered.

"Manfrengensen," the man replied. "It is quite a difficult name, so please, just call me 'Clyde.'"

"Um, okay then…um…Mr. Clyde. I don't really have experience working in a morgue. I have pretty much just worked at a no-kill animal shelter. But there are similarities, I think. There was a lot of paperwork to do, and I had to talk with people who were adopting pets to be in their forever homes, so…y'know…I can talk to people. Oh, and if this job requires any…um… clean-up…let me assure you that I have had to clean up pretty much anything you can think of. From vomit to piss to blood to…well, I guess you can imagine. Anyway, I'm pretty smart and I can pick up on stuff pretty quickly and I'm really excited to begin a new career if you could just give me a chance."

"I see, I see," Clyde began again. "And, please, let me ask you, since you are obviously quite fond of animals, why are you leaving that position and why have you applied to work here in our...heh, heh, heh...*warm* and *inviting* little corner of the world?"

Huh. This dude actually has a sense of humor. Dry as hell, but... Arima thought to herself before responding to the question. "Well, the animal shelter was forced to relocate from its current building. I guess it's being torn down to make way for condos or a shopping center or something. There are a lot of grand old historical buildings there that are going to be demolished, which I think is very sad. Anyway, the new location is too far away. I don't have a car because I've never really needed one and it would take over an hour on the bus, so I had to leave there. And why this job? Well, I'm not gonna lie to you. It pays way more than my previous one and my Grams- I mean, my grandmother- wanted me to find something that had benefits like health insurance and a retirement plan. Not that I need it right now. I'm only twenty-three. But she wanted me to have some financial stability, I guess. And as far as the actual job, y'know, I'm kinda a night owl, anyway, and I figured this was a job that I could learn without much...um...effort, I guess."

Arima then began hearing whispers in the furthest corner of her mind.

Come see! Come See!

What? What is it?

There is one! Right in there! One who can hear us!

Really? One that can help us move on and leave this horribly boring place? A chance to move on from sitting and watching other souls go to Enlightenment while we are stuck here?

Yes! Yes! We must make contact with her!

"Very good," Clyde began once again. "I suppose that answer is as good as any I have heard. And honest. I like that. Not many people dream of working overnight in a morgue. So, do you frighten easily? Some have said is it downright *creepy* down here in the...heh, heh, heh...dead of night, being surrounded by corpses."

Arima began sweating profusely as her eyes darted around at the bare concrete walls and she heard, *Oh! What a grand question.*

Yes, it will be quite interesting to see how she answers this. Just how easily are you to scare, deary?

"Uh…uh…uh…" Arima began stuttering before tightly closing her eyes for a moment in order to block out the formless voices and focus on her answer. "Uh…no, not usually. I'm really into horror movies, so it takes quite a bit to shock me. And there's no such thing as zombies…I think. But recently I…um…no, I think I'll be fine."

Fine! She says she will be fine!

Oh, she doesn't know what she has in store for her. We'll see if she can make it through a night. Then we'll see how fine she is, heh, heh, heh.

"Very well," Clyde replied. "One more question, and this is most important. Have you ever had or thought about having sex with a dead person?"

"Wha…wha…*what? Eeeewww!*" Arima exclaimed as her mind thought, *Although there was that guy a couple years ago who just laid there like a dead fish, but he did have a heartbeat…I think.*

Clyde looked up at Arima for the first time with a broad smile on his face. "Well, I shall take your reaction as a 'no.' Very good. You may be surprised if you knew just how many night staff I have had to fire because of such…um…activities. Oh, my, there was an incident several years ago where two college girls died of alcohol poisoning at the same party. The night watchman…um…let's just say he took advantage of the still-warm bodies and made quite a mess. It was quite disgusting and, of course, we had to involve the authorities. That is one of our little sayings around here… 'If it is a corpse you want to nail, then your ass is going to jail!' Oh, and another one is, 'You are not allowed to screw any body that is blue!' I thought that I would make rhymes of it, so that people would remember should they feel any…um…urges. You would be wise to keep this in mind."

I think she's kind of cute, Arima heard the male spirit's voice say. *I don't know that I would have minded if she had wanted to take a ride on my body. Y'know. Before it was buried.*

Oh, my lord! We may be dead, but we are still married. I am so tired of watching you ogle the living females that come in here!

C'mon honey. It's not like I can do anything with them. Lighten up.

It is the intention that matters, not the act. The intention itself is a betrayal to me and to our vows. Now, you just think about that!

Oh, I will! Right after I think about picking you up from that sleazy hotel the night we died!

"Uh…uh…uh…okay then," Arima stuttered. "So…will you get back to me, or…"

"Why yes!" Clyde replied with surprising excitement. "I'll get back to you right now! When can you start? I have a very good feeling about you."

"Uh…yeah. Great. I can start right away," Arima excitedly exclaimed. "And… you won't regret this. I'll show up every night and I'll always be on time, and I'll keep all of these spirits who are trapped here in line!"

Arima clasped her mouth as she realized what she had just blurted out. Clyde just stared at her for a moment before letting out a slight snorting snicker and said, "Oh…and a sense of humor to boot! Yes, you will fit in just fine here. We are focused on our business at hand, but…well, just between you and me, we *do* like to *cut up* every now and again, heh, heh, heh. Oh, dear. Where is that form? Excuse me for a moment, won't you? I need to go to another office and get a form. I swore I had made enough copies. Why do these things keep coming up missing?"

As soon as Clyde left the room, Arima looked upward at the ceiling and said quietly, "Listen, you two. We're going to have to co-exist with each other down here. And I'm telling you right now, that if you do *anything* to get me in trouble, I will…well… I'm not sure yet what I can do, but you will not like it. So, do not give me any shit, all right?"

Jeez, she's a bit moody, isn't she, dear? the female spirit stated.

Why, yes, she is. All right, Arima. We won't give you any trouble. But we will *want your help to move on in return, deal?*

"Uh…sure. Don't know how I can be of help, but…um…sure. What are your names?"

The female spirit replied, *You may address us as "Mr. and Mrs. Roper."*

"Sorry, folks, no karaoke tonight. We still can't connect to the Internet," the DJ announced from the stage as Jessie West broke down once again in uncontrollable sobbing. Her loving husband, Cliff, just held her as her blonde hair bounced with every exhalation of grief. His high school football jersey was saturated in her tears as he listened to the next announcement.

Louise Azar's voice came booming through the PA system. "Ladies and gentlemen! Please welcome my most beloved granddaughter and wish her a happy birthday!"

Arima was encased in smiles and hugs from her friends and family, and she was placed at a table in the middle of the dance floor. The plastic top was removed from the dish in the middle of the table and Arima began to drool. The candles were lit on the stack of brownies and the group burst out into a jovial version of "Happy Birthday To You." Arima stared at the stack of flickering brownies in anticipation of taking her first bite and procuring her first step toward a well-earned buzz when she heard two unfamiliar male voices singing much more loudly and with a much more pronounced slur than the rest of the group.

She looked up at them. They were two brawny, hairy men clinging to one another and their gold shirts were unbuttoned down to their protruding bellies. Both had finely trimmed beards. One had naturally silver-grey hair. The other probably did as well, but it was covered by a ghastly black dye job.

Arima blew out the candles and made a wish. *I wish to get the greatest buzz of my life tonight. And maybe get laid. But mainly the buzz. Thanks.* Only one of those wishes would come true on this particular evening. She took her first bite of a brownie, and her first wish was on its way to being fulfilled.

"Hey Jessie, Cliff," Arima said as she tentatively approached two of her best friends and housemates. "Sorry that the internet thing still isn't working. I'm sure they'll get it…" Arima was cut off as Jessie went screaming into the bathroom.

"Dammit, Arima. I know you meant well, but…I just got her out of there. Jessie! Sweetie! It'll all be okay! When we get home, you can write down all of your posts you want to send! I'll like them, I promise! I'll draw a bunch of little thumbs ups! Please sweetie! Please come out of the bathroom!"

Arima rolled her eyes and sighed as she went up to her closest friend and confidant, Jamie, who was loudly laughing with the brawny pair of overexaggerated singers. "Arima! My love! Come and meet my new friends!" Jamie declared as she embraced Arima, forcing her face between Jamie's recently acquired breasts.

"I…can't…breathe!" Arima cried out before releasing herself from Jamie's clutches. "Seriously, Jamie. I know you always wanted a great rack, but those things are ridiculous!"

"Oh, we'll see how ridiculous they are later tonight when I have that man's face covered with them!"

Arima looked over at the slightly built, plaid-shirt-and-blue-jeans-wearing cowboy in the corner. "Uh…I don't think so. He looks straight to me."

Jamie and her two new friends burst out laughing. "Oh, deary," the black-dyed-haired man gushed. "They may all *look* straight. But *trust* me. They most certainly are not *all* straight! Now just what do you think that a man that looks like *that* is looking for in a place like *this*? Well, sweetie, he is looking for someone like *me*. But his dirty little conscience thinks that that is wrong, so he will end up with someone like *her* and rationalize that it isn't wrong if he is with a woman that just *happens* to have the *real* equipment that he so desires!"

"Oh, my lord. Must you *always* be so vulgar?" the silver-haired man responded. "And I would remind the two of you to tread lightly with that man. He may become offended at too much of a flirtation, just as straight women are rightfully offended by too much of an overture from a straight man. It is no different. Do not assume that every buck you see is down for a…well, roll in the hay. It is pompous and arrogant of you just as it is in the straight world."

"Really? But I'm fabulous!" Jamie declared. "Yes, you are, girlfriend!" exclaimed the darker haired man.

"Yes, you are," came the moderating voice of the silver-haired man. "But not everyone will think so and not everyone desires you. We would all, straight, gay, or otherwise, do well to remember that. We make a pass. See if we catch their eye. If not, we move on. That is being respectful to another human being. That is all that I have to say on this matter."

The dark-haired man squealed out in delight and declared, "Oh, my god! You are *so* sexy when you lecture me! Now give Papa Bear a big kiss!"

"Okay," Arima replied with disinterest as she stared at these two embracing men through her increasingly bloodshot eyes. "So, who *are* you guys?"

"Oh, my dearies, I am *soooo* sorry!" Jamie exclaimed. *This* dark haired brute is Paciano and *this* silver fox is Stellan! Aren't their names just wonderful and exotic? The name 'Stellan' is Swedish and means 'peaceful one.' And 'Paciano' is Spanish and means 'peace.' It was as though they were meant to find one another! Isn't it just so romantically delicious? And they have just been married and are here on their honeymoon! Oh, how *overjoyed* I am to have found you two. You are an inspiration. Tell me. When do you have to return to New York?"

Louise Azar interrupted at that moment and said, "Excuse me, gentlemen, but may I borrow my granddaughter for a moment?"

Louise took Arima by the hand and sat her at a corner booth at the far end of the bar. "Arima, please listen to me. Those two seem like fine men, but they are from New York. They may be the lure that will lead you to involvement with the copper-headed demon. I am asking you to please just steer clear of those two. Just to be safe, all right?"

"Awwww, Grams," Arima replied as she stared at her hands and contemplated the miracle that was the movement of her fingers. "They're just a couple of fun guys here on their honeymoon. I'll probably never see them again. Nothin' to get worked up over. Hey, are there any more brownies?"

"Yes, there are. But before that, I must know. Did anyone or…anything… try to make a connection with you today at the morgue?"

Arima burst out in a giggle and stated loudly, "Did anyone reach out to me? Oh, Grams! I'm gonna *love* this gig. Let me tell you about the Ropers!"

Chapter 5

Well...Hello, There, Handsome

Arima arrived one hour before her shift on her first night at the morgue for her mandatory training session. She entered the meeting room down the hall from the morgue and took her seat on a hard plastic chair behind a well-worn metal folding table. She looked around the room. *Wow. They really don't believe in decorating around here, do they?* she thought to herself as she read the Workplace Rules posters regarding harassment, safety, and emergency procedures that were clinging to the grey concrete walls with tape. *Man, this job is going to be so boring. I wonder if maybe I could just take a hit once in a while?* she mused before her eyes widened at the broad image coming through the door.

Her bored expression was immediately replaced by a wide smile as a tall, handsome-faced, somewhat portly Black man entered the room. The shirt tail of his light blue button-up shirt was halfway out of his faded blue jeans. He looked somewhat disheveled and slovenly. To Arima, he looked ideal. He took his place at the front of the room and smiled.

"Hey, there," he said. "Welcome to our little slice of heaven. My name is Marcus. Marcus Jefferson. I usually work the second shift and I'll be your trainer tonight. And if you have any questions, feel free to call me any time. My number's on the call list in the office."

Oh, I think I'm gonna have a lot *of questions,* Arima thought as she noticed the striking man's unencumbered left ring finger.

"So, please. What is your name?" Marcus asked with a tone of genuine interest.

"Me?" Arima immediately stammered, "I mean...of course, me. Heh. I'm the only one here. Sorry, um...I'm Arima Azan and I just want to say how thankful I am for this opportunity."

"Uh, yeah, cool," a slightly confused Marcus replied. "But you don't have to kiss my ass. I'm a working stiff just like you. Get it? Working *stiff*? Just one of our little jokes around here. And really, you don't have to kiss anybody's ass. Not even Clyde's. He's a pretty cool dude. He just wants us to show up, do our jobs, and not make waves. He's pretty low key. You don't even have to laugh at his jokes, although I've been here for three years now, and I have to admit, sometimes I kinda chuckle at them. Wow. That's pretty sad because his jokes are so awful. Maybe it's a sign that I need to move on, huh?"

No! No! No! You can't go anywhere! Arima's voice in her head screamed out at him. "Uh, no. I think that...um...you're where you belong right now. I mean...well, I mean...you have to get me trained up, right?"

"Oh, yeah!" Marcus yelled out. "That's why I'm in here tonight! Man, I gotta admit, this job is overall pretty boring. It's even worse now that the wireless Internet has been taken down by terrorists or somethin'. Can't even pass the time watching po-...I mean, playing on my phone. So, when I get really bored, I just kinda...y'know...take a puff. Not much. Just enough to, y'know, take the edge off. Then I eat a lot of candy and chips."

Arima's heart melted as she thought to herself, *Oh, my God. I'm in love.*

Marcus went into his training. He covered safety procedures, emergency procedures, delivery intake, miscellaneous forms and the corpse filing system. Arima clung to his every word while simultaneously not learning anything. The intended hour-long training took Marcus eighteen minutes before he said, "Well, just one more thing in here. You gotta watch this video on the legal shit around having sex with corpses. They take that pretty seriously. Then we'll tour the morgue, all right?"

"All right," Arima replied dreamily. Marcus turned out the buzzing fluorescent overhead lights and turned on the twenty-year-old flatscreen TV. As the nine-minute epic training video entitled *Digging Your Own Grave: An Introduction to the Legal Consequences of Having Intercourse with Expired Humans*, began flickering on the screen, Arima gazed over at her handsome trainer and began fantasizing about what she would like to do to- or with-him. She gazed back at the TV and thought, *If they don't want us to have sex in here, why did they make all of the corpses in this video so damn hot?*

The video ended and Marcus turned the lights back on. The overhead bulbs began buzzing once again as Marcus asked, "Okay, so that's about it, any questions?"

"Nope," Arima immediately replied. "I think I've got it. Don't play with the stiffs on the stiffs. Got it."

Marcus looked at Arima with bewildered eyes before bursting out laughing. "Oh, man! That was classic! You're gonna do just fine here. You gotta tell that one to Clyde in the morning!"

They entered the morgue and Arima immediately heard the spirit of Mr. Roper.

She's here! She's come back!

Who is here? Oh, your new little human fantasy. Isn't that nice?

Oh, like you don't dream about our Marcus there?

Well, of course I do! But I can't make contact with him. I can't interact with him the way you can with Arima, so it is completely different!

Wasn't so different the night we...

The Ropers bickering ceased when Arima said to them under her breath, "Would you two just pipe down?"

"Excuse me?" Marcus asked as he turned around from opening one of the morgue corpse drawers.

"Oh, um, nothin'," an embarrassed Arima hastily replied. "I was just sayin'...um...aren't you so wise now."

"Wise? Me?" Marcus replied with a chuckle. "Well, that's not somethin' I get accused of often. I don't know how wise I've been in my twenty-five years. It wasn't so wise to drop outta high school. Nope. That little trick got me kicked out of the house. Moms and Pops love me, but they were tired of me pullin' pranks and shit, so they decided to teach me a lesson. And they did. Kicked me out on my eighteenth birthday, right after I dropped out. So, I pretty much just couch- surfed for a few years and got fired from every job I had. They were just too boring, or the manager was a prick or somethin', y'know? But they always had me over for Sunday dinner after we all went to church together. They kept tryin' to get me to be responsible. To take life seriously. I just never really listened. I never did anything really *bad*, but I never did anything really *good* either. I was young and selfish. That all changed when..."

Marcus's voice trailed off and he looked away to hide the tears that were forming in his eyes. He had known Arima for less than an hour but felt as though she was a kindred soul that he could open up to. He looked back at her with his eyes filled with tears. Arima immediately wished to be able to embrace him and absorb whatever pain it was that he was experiencing at that moment.

"Sorry, I didn't mean to get all gushy and shit," Marcus stated sheepishly as he looked down at his well-worn canvas tennis shoes. "It's just that, a few years ago, I had to grow up. You see, my Moms got herself some cancer. It's pretty bad and she's so weak usually that she can't work anymore. And my Pops just couldn't keep up with all the bills and everything. So I buckled down and settled into this job. They let me move back home and most of my paycheck goes to keeping the household up. Y'know, the mortgage, bills, food. That way, Pops can afford to get the care that Moms needs, so… y'know…she can stay with us. I've learned that there are more important things in life than our own personal needs. I've learned that we all need to lean on one another sometimes to make this world work."

The urge to hug Marcus became overwhelming and Arima extended her arms and enveloped his frame with hers. She felt his body tense, then immediately relax as he accepted this emotional respite from his newfound friend. She concentrated and could feel his pain being absorbed into her soul. She focused harder and envisioned his pain being consumed by burning flames. She heard him let out a relieved exhalation and the hurtfulness dissipated for the both of them as she felt his pain turn to harmless ashes.

Arima relinquished her embrace and said reservedly, "Um…sorry, I guess that wasn't very professional of me. I just thought…I mean…I just wanted to…"

"No, no, no," Marcus immediately replied. "It's okay. Thank you. That was probably the best hug that I've ever had. Like, you made all my hurt go away. I guess I just needed a hug in that moment and you were there for me".

And I always will be, Arima thought to herself before hearing the Ropers say to her in a childish sing-song voice,

Arima's got a boyfriend, Arima's got a boyfriend, Arima's got a…

"Just shut up!" Arima yelled out.

"Uh, ok, sorry," a surprised Marcus responded.

"No, not you," Arima hastily replied. Her mind raced as she wondered whether she could confide in him about her newfound talents. After all, he had just opened up to her. They just had an intense emotional connection. Perhaps he wouldn't think that she was crazy. On the other hand...

Arima began chuckling and said, "Not *you*. I wasn't talking to *you*. It's just...um...sometimes when I get kinda emotional I get thoughts in my head, and I tell them to shut up. I just got caught up in the moment and forgot where I was. Sorry."

"Yeah, you got emotional?" Marcus asked tenderly as he gazed into Arima's mahogany eyes for the first time.

"Delivery time!" came the exclamation from the police officer who was wheeling in a newly deceased corpse. "Got a fresh one for ya straight from the autopsy. Real piece of work, this one. Had to be gunned down after a standoff with us. Was chanting all kinds of weird religious and racist shit. The world's better off, if ya ask me. Here, sign this".

Marcus showed her how to check in and "file" the corpse. They awkwardly chuckled to one another as Marcus said, "Well, I guess I should go now, but listen. If you need anything and I mean *anything*, I'm just a phone call away, okay? And Clyde will be in around seven. He'll probably come in a little early on your first few nights, just to check up on you, all right?"

"Yeah, all right," Arima dreamily replied.

Marcus left the room and Arima began skipping around in a large circle on the cold concrete floor while giggling.

So, Arima, Mrs. Roper's voice echoed in her head. *How does it feel to be in love?*

Yes, Arima. Pretty good first day on the job, I would say.

Yes, dear. Remember when we were first in love? Just look at her face. How I wish I had never allowed that look to go off of my face.

Me, too, dear, me, too. We both made so many mistakes all those years ago. And now, our children are devoid of love in their hearts. We must talk to them. We must...

Mr. Roper's voice was cut off by a dark eerie presence emerging from the recently closed drawer. The fluorescent lights remained on, but became encased in a dark purple shroud, causing the entire room to darken in a sinister purplish hue.

Arima began hyperventilating as she could feel the dark presence swirling around her soul, looking for an entrance.

Oh, no, Mr. Roper stated mournfully. *It's one of those. So many more of those here recently. Arima, stay away from him. Do not let him in. He is dangerous to you. To us. Just let him pull his pranks and stay out of it.*

Shut up, you two. The sinister spirit's low, gravelly voice came emanating from the dark purple mist that could only be seen by Arima and The Ropers.

I won't be trapped here forever. I will be sent for. I will rise again in another form and continue to do the bidding of the great Vetis, the Tempter of the Holy! Those mortals have no idea that they have made me stronger! More powerful! All I need is a vessel to consume. A weak-minded medium to absorb my spirit and transfer it into another.

Arima's hyperventilation continued, and her eyes rolled back into her head. She began violently shaking as she elevated off of the floor.

The demonic spirit began cackling as he gleefully watched Arima's seizing body floating helplessly.

Ah, I see that I have found one already. Oh, you can hear me, can't you? Good. Well, listen up, bitch. If you want to survive. If you do not wish to perish, then you shall do exactly as I tell you. Because if you don't, I will shred your flesh from your body. I shall feast upon your organs. I will kill you so slowly that by the end, you will be begging for me to let you die. And then, once you finally do die, I will do the same thing to your soul. I shall murder you in the most violent ways over and over again for all eternity. Or...you can let me in and transfer me to the next human that walks through that door. The choice is yours. You got that- n****r?

Chapter 6

You Probably Shouldn't Have Said That

"Oh! *Hell,* no! I am *not* putting up with any racist shit from some deplorable spirit!" Arima screamed out at the swirling smog. "You want in? You want me to take your soul in and transfer you into someone else so you can continue your racist bullshit on this earth? That really what you want? All right, then. C'mon in here, cracker".

The devilish spirit cackled in delight as Arima instinctively opened her soul to his.

No, Arima! Don't! Mrs. Roper's spirit pleaded.

Don't do it, Arima. He is too powerful. He will use you and your body for horrible things. Do not let him in! Mr. Roper added.

"Yeah?" a smirking Arima replied. "You think so? I think that this little worm doesn't know *what* he is going up against".

And then she felt it. She felt him penetrate her. She elevated off of the ground as her eyes rolled back into her head and she once again began violently seizing.

Heh, heh, heh. Thanks bitch, the sinister presence stated as he entered the warmth of Arima's being. *You think you can go up against me? Here. Let me show you a few things.*

Her mind began projecting images as though she were sitting in a movie theatre. They were blurry at first. Just a mix of disembodied colors mixing in with one another. Then the images began coming into focus until they were crystal clear. Arima was repulsed by them.

There were three white men with shaven heads. They were wearing tattered and stained blue jeans and brown short-sleeved shirts. Their arms and necks were scarred by tattoos of ignorant hate. They had a young Black girl surrounded. She could not have been more than twelve years old. She was pleading with them to stop. To let her go. Tears streamed down her innocent face as her anguished pleas continued.

With every begging sentence that she uttered, the sadistic men laughed harder. They tore at her clothes. They slapped her in the face. They brutally punched and kicked her in her abdomen, ribs, and back. The cackling trio circled her mercilessly as the child was forced to absorb the never-ending blows. She was thrown to the ground and her underpants were ripped from her flailing legs.

Arima's soul screamed out in anguish as she witnessed that which no human being, especially a child, should ever have to experience. It was the most depraved action that anyone could ever take against another. It was brutal. It was disgusting. It was sadistic. It was the vile actions of the small, weak-willed, and weak-minded. It was the actions of people who have no regard for the sanctity of another's rights or dignity. Who have no regard for the sanctity of life itself. Arima's soul began to warm and expand as she realized for the first time that those who hold no sanctity for life should carry no expectations of continuing theirs. They had waived that right through their brutality of others. They are, indeed, deplorable. And they should die.

The depraved spirit howled with laughter as he showed Arima the final scene. The young girl's corpse was hanging from a flashing stop sign. Her battered, naked body was morbidly illuminated by flashing red, revealing multiple bruises and deep lacerations. One of her broken ribs was protruding from her side. A small red flag with a swastika had been hung from it. Her innocent face was gashed open and her formerly brilliant eyes were swollen shut. Her lips had been bitten off. The "men's" vile semen slithered down her tender thighs.

Arima was a lover of all things horror. Movies, books, comics. She loved it all. She loved the thrill she got from a jump scare or the creepy vibes that caused goosebumps as she read about demonic possession. But that was fiction. That was she, as a viewer, safely expunging her darker thoughts through watching the fictional violence of others. She, and her horror-loving friends, could absolve themselves of feeling guilt about their darker impulses by living vicariously through the fabricated violence of others. It was nothing more than thrill-seeking entertainment in the comfort of her own home. No one was ever *really* injured in any way. The horror that she watched and read was fake. The screams were fake. The blood was fake. The trauma was fake. The death was fake.

This, however, was all too real, Arima realized. This had actually *happened*. This was *actually happening* at this very moment to some other innocent person. At this very moment, some innocent child was pleading for the pain to stop. This was the true horror of actual life for far too many of our sisters and brothers. This was the barbarous horror that even fiction writers dared not discuss, because it is too taboo, too dark, and too brutal for even the most desensitized viewer. But by our choosing to not shine a bright spotlight on the true horrors in our world, we allow it to grow. To continue. To thrive. For generation after generation after generation. Brutality of others cannot be swept under the rug. It cannot be wished away. It cannot be prayed away. It must be exposed in the same graphic way that it had been experienced in order for it to be truly understood and felt to our core. We must *see* the innocent school children whose bodies have been torn apart by the bullets of a coward. We must *see* the tortured bodies of murder victims. We must *see* the torn-apart bodies of the innocent civilian victims of our brutal wars. We must *hear* the stories of physical and mental trauma caused by sexual assault and harassment. Arima finally understood that we cannot allow ourselves to become complacent about the world's *true* horrors that seem so distant to most of us. For if we do, those *true* horrors very well may be inflicted upon us and our own loved ones. We must acknowledge the reality of it. The senselessness of it. The sadistic brutality of it. The inhumanity of it. We must shed a genuine empathetic tear. And then, the horror must be confronted. And it must be confronted with the same amount of force and brutality with which it was originally inflicted by soulless trash.

Heh, heh, heh. And that was all it took to rid an entire neighborhood of the Black infestation of vermin like you. You see now, don't you, bitch? the arrogant spirit whispered into Arima's soul. *You see what you're up against now, don't you? And if you do not place me in an another's able body, I will do to your soul what I did to that kid's body. You have seen how I can make your body convulse.*

And that is without much effort. Just imagine the pain that I can inflict if I put my mind to it. I will rape and torture you until you beg me to die. And once you die, I will simply wait for another like you to come along and force them to do my bidding. Now be the good slave girl that you were put here to be. Just walk outside onto the street. I'll tell you when the right one comes along. Do it...now!

Arima's body stopped convulsing as she descended until her canvas-adorned feet touched the floor. Her eyes rolled back into their natural position and were opened. Her deep mahogany pupils were raging with a glimmering fire that she had never experienced before.

What...what are you...how did you do that? I didn't release you! the disheveled spirit stuttered out in confusion.

Arima furled her brow, wiped the drool from her lips and smiled devilishly before saying, "Now, asshole you are going to listen to *me*. I may be new to this game, but it's like I just instinctively now know what I can and can't do. And I know that you are *far* too weak and pathetic to have any control over me. I *allowed* you to do those things to my body, but I was in complete control of it the entire time. I *allowed* you to show me those horrendous images, but I could have stopped them at any time. I didn't because I needed to know. I needed to experience it. I needed to feel it. And I do now know. I now know that there is true evil in this world that must be vanquished. And I now know the name of that sweet girl. *And* the names of your accomplices."

"Now, let me correct you on a couple things. For starters, there are probably demonic spirits of the followers of Vetis who *can* control me if I allow them in. Who can take over my body and soul and force me to do terrible things. I guess that is the curse that I carry for being made of equal parts of my sweet mother *and* my sadistic father. But *you* do not possess that power. I could sense it from the first moment that I met you. How does it feel to have a girl of Jamaican descent with brown skin wield *far* more power than your impotent Aryan shell of a self?

"And another point of clarification. There may be some women who can transfer spirits from their bodies into another living body. I don't know about that. All that I know is that I can allow spirits in and allow them to use my body to try to redeem themselves so that they may move on to Enlightenment. And I can transfer those spirits. I can expel them from me back into the vast nothingness of their current hell that they are trapped in.

Or I can transfer them into inanimate objects. And that is just what I will now do to you."

"Let's see here. Where to put a low-life scumbag like you? Heh, heh, heh. Oh, I know."

Where are we going? Where are you taking me? Talk to me, bitch! the demon screamed out at Arima as she walked out of the morgue, down the hallway, and into the meeting room where she had received her training.

"You are a part of the master race, huh?" Arima stated haughtily. "Yeah, I don't think so because *I* am now the master of *you*. Enjoy your reading for all of eternity, you sick bastard!"

Arima concentrated and began expunging the demonic one from her being. She could feel his brittle nails scraping against her soul as he attempted in vain to cling to her essence. She concentrated further and heard his anguished wail as his spirit was permanently placed into the Workplace Harassment poster.

She chuckled to herself as she read the parts of the poster that she felt were most fitting for this impotent worm of an entity.

HARRASSMENT WILL NOT BE TOLERATED!

It is our company policy to provide a safe workplace. We will not tolerate any form of harassment.

Examples of Harassment:

- Verbal abuse- shouting, yelling, swearing, name calling, and vulgarity.
- Threats or physical abuse.
- Intimidation or manipulation.
- Cruel comments, belittling, or insults.
- Aggressive behavior.
- Sexual harassment, unwanted touching, or stalking
- Unequal treatment due to race, gender, age, size, religion, sexual orientation, gender identity, or country of origin.

"I suggest you read that carefully," Arima stated boldly as she stood in front of the poster like a conquering hero. "I *will not* tolerate any harassment from *you*. But *you*, on the other hand, will be subjected to an *eternity* of harassment from *me*, so you better keep your damned filthy mouth shut!"

Arima returned to the morgue and flopped her frame upon the wheeled office chair in front of her desk. She lazily pulled a fresh joint from her breast pocket, lit it, and inhaled deeply. "Ahhh…that's the stuff," she stated in a quiet satisfied voice before picking up the receiver of the phone.

Who are you calling Arima? Mrs. Roper inquired.

"The cops. I gotta tell them who murdered that poor little girl," Arima replied flatly before explaining to the Ropers the horrendous images that she had been shown.

But what will you tell them Arima? Mr. Roper replied. *What will you tell them as to how you know all of this? Will you tell them the truth? Do you think that they will believe you? No, dear. Put the phone down. The others must be dealt with in another way.*

"But how?" Arima cried out.

You know how, dear, Mrs. Roper answered. *They must be dealt with in a much more permanent manner. And then, you can place them with their cowardly friend in the poster. That was quite clever my dear. To place the spirit of a misogynistic, xenophobic, racist into a Workplace Harassment poster to torment him for all of eternity. I am beginning to really like you, my dear.*

"What? *Kill them?*" Arima cried out to the seemingly blank walls. "I can't *kill them*! I would *never* be able to do that! It's just not in me! But you have a point. They need to be taken out by someone. Jeez. Knowing a vigilante serial killer right now sure would come in handy. But, like, someone like *that* really exists in this world. It's absurd. Any other ideas you two?"

Yes. I believe that I might have a solution to your little problem, Mrs. Roper answered.

No, dear, not him, Mr. Roper quickly responded.

Yes. Him. Arima, dear, there is another spirit who has been trapped here for some time that you have not yet met. He keeps to himself, and it may take some coaxing to draw him out, but I believe that he may be able to help you. He prefers to be known as the Botanist.

Chapter 7

I Picked These Just for You

Herbert Jenkins, who would later be known simply as "the Botanist," was a pathetically weak individual from the moment his meager cry emerged from his mother's body. As a child, he was always awkward around other people, especially other children who would ridicule him mercilessly for his gangly frame and beak-like hooked nose that protruded from between his constantly blinking, beady eyes.

Herbert had no friends, except for his doting mother. His father had been killed in action during World War I just prior to his birth and his mother, whose appearance was just as homely as her son's, never remarried. The pair would spend their evenings listening to their favorite radio programs or playing in their lavish garden behind their modest, but well-kept one-bedroom bungalow in New Orleans.

Herbert would spend hour upon blissful hour in their family garden, tending to his plants as though they were his own children. Over the years, he built the garden into a local showcase that traveling green thumbs would tour. They would gaze in amazement at the majesty of his creation. The various shades of green and textures of the leaves that would joyously blend together. The multiple colors and shapes of the delicate petals that overlapped one another as though their blooms were in loving embraces throughout the yard. The prisms that were created as the morning sun's rays penetrated the modest dew drops that clung to the flora. It was all quite spectacular and overwhelming for the throngs of visitors that arrived to tour on a nearly daily basis.

And standing in the middle of it all, as the amazed tourists made their way through the kaleidoscopic yard, was a beaming Herbert. This was his creation. This was his world. And it was the only place where he found acceptance, if not outright affection, from other people. In *his* world, he was not ugly. He was not ridiculed. He was enveloped with the love and adoration of others. This is where Herbert was home.

It was the exact opposite in his school. Herbert would frequently attempt to feign illness to skip school, but his mother usually saw through his ruse and would make him get up and get dressed, often in ill-fitting shirts and pants that had fit the rapidly growing boy just a few months prior.

He would be subjected to endless ridicule as his lanky frame, which was typically a foot taller than his classmates, strode down the school's hallways. He was called many names, including "honker," "flood," and "crane." The most hurtful to Herbert was when he was called "flower girl" as this was not just an attack upon his person, but also towards his beloved friends in his garden.

By junior high school, Herbert would frequently be caught dreamily gazing at a pretty classmate from across the room. The young lady would be all too happy to tell her boyfriend about the perceived slight. And the boyfriend, in turn, would be only too happy to pummel Herbert after school. Herbert would limp home with his shirt torn, dirty, and bloody. His face would carry multiple purplish bruises and his small eyes would be blackened and swollen. He would open the gate of the white picket fence and go around the house and be enveloped by his world. He would sit in the middle of his majestic garden and cry. He would then go to a certain area in the back of the garden near his tool shed. This area of his world was his most cherished as it housed plants that held the capability of healing. He would use the oils from his dearest friends to treat his wounds. Herbert had learned not only how to plant and tend for his flowers. He was now beginning to experiment and learn about the medicinal benefits that many flowers possessed. His flowers depended upon him for their survival. And he depended upon them for his.

By high school, Herbert had become conditioned to avoid any contact with his female classmates. It was simply too painful for him. The pain would either be physical and come from a jealous boyfriend eager to show "his girl" his male dominance or, more frequently, would be emotional as he would see the mockingly cruel expression upon a young lady's face as he would give her an innocent smile. Although these female wonders looked as beautiful and delicate as his beloved flowers, he resigned himself to believing that females did not contain nectar or sweet-smelling pollen. To the contrary, to Herbert, women were poisonous.

Although brilliant in the sciences, especially chemistry and, of course, botany, he was emotionally insecure and immature and did not understand how gender played no role in personality type. And he did not understand how peer pressure affected his classmates. If a female were ever to be kind to him, then she would be met with the same cruel treatment that he was receiving. So even the most kindhearted of classmates would simply avoid him. Herbert also lacked the social skills to try to endear himself to others in other ways to counter his awkward appearance. He was not handsome. He had little to no personality. He had no physical strength or athletic aptitude. So, in the world of young romance, he had no chance.

Beginning in high school, Herbert firmly believed that most people were uncaring and cruel, and this was especially true of women. He would live his life alone and love and be loved by his cherished plants and his endearing mother. He would ironically use his intellectual prowess to harness the medicinal power of his friends to help other people recover from their assorted maladies. This would be his contribution to his species that contributed nothing to him.

This outlook dramatically changed in the spring of 1952. Herbert, now 34 and working in a pharmaceutical laboratory, saw the most beautiful vision that his constantly blinking, beady eyes had ever seen. The young woman was a recent graduate with a master's degree and had gained employment as Herbert's assistant. Her pale skin seemed to glow as the sun's rays beamed upon her through the laboratory's window. Her golden hair cascaded over her delicate shoulders and framed her brilliant blue eyes. Her smile was reminiscent of a brilliant red rose petal as it began to open. Her figure was slim and her hips and behind were tightly enveloped in a knee-length pencil skirt. Her calves were stretched and accentuated to perfection by her three-inch high black leather pumps and sheer stockings. And little was left to the imagination as her tight, short-sleeved light pink sweater clung to her shapely breasts. Herbert wondered to himself if God had ever created someone or something this perfect.

Herbert had his answer the moment the young woman opened her lips to introduce herself. The answer was "no." This was the most perfect creature that God had ever created. His heart opened and years of bitterness melted away as she smiled at him demurely. She spoke to him. She listened to him. There was never a trace of repulsion toward him upon her angelic face. She looked upon him as they spoke together as ideally and non-judgmentally as his cherished flowers in his garden. She responded to his meek attempts at humor with light giggles, a hair flip, and a light touch upon his boney shoulder. He felt goosebumps and slightly woozy as he experienced the first delicate touch of a woman in his life. She was intoxicating.

The pair quickly forged a strong and slightly flirtatious working relationship as Herbert educated her on the various experimental plant-based treatments that he was working on. Each morning he would bring her coffee exactly as she liked it. One cream, two sugars. They would eat lunch together in the facility cafeteria and she would lightly brush his foot with hers while ignoring the bewildered expressions of their on-looking co-workers.

Herbert began bringing her presents, especially after she would casually mention a certain piece of jewelry or dress or shoes that she had seen window shopping. She could never afford such extravagances, she would tell him, but she enjoyed dreaming about how she might have them some day. Herbert took it upon himself to make all of her dreams come true, so over the next few weeks the presents became increasingly expensive. And her response to the presents would become increasingly gracious as she began giving the love-stricken suitor a provocative peck on his pasty cheek.

He would beam with titillated pleasure as she would come to work wearing the dress, broach, earrings, or bejeweled ring that he had given her the day before. His bank account was dwindling, but his heart was exploding from the rapturous delight of his first love. He was convinced that this wondrous personification of perfection would be his bride someday.

Herbert felt that this was the one person in the world that he could open up to. He told her about his garden and how it was his most cherished place in all of the world. He told her how his garden made him feel accepted and loved. He told her how his garden made him feel whole. He then told her that she made him feel the same way and that he was falling in love with her. He handed her a voluminous bouquet of his most cherished flowers from his most cherished place on the earth. To him, it was the most loving and thoughtful gift that he could bestow upon her. The combination of the various scents of the flowers was overwhelmingly sweet and beautiful. She looked at his teary eyes and sincere expression with loving admiration as her blue eyes sparkled under the neon lights in the laboratory. She smiled sweetly, gave him a quick peck upon his cheek, took the flowers and excused herself. Before leaving the room, she looked back at him and gave him a not-so-subtle wink and shake of her rump.

She was gone for quite a while. He thought that he had heard her voice coming from outside of an open window. He could not make out what was being said until he went to the opened window and leaned his ear toward the screen. He heard another female co-worker ask what she had received from him that day. His love responded by saying "just these." He then heard two female voices along with that of a male co-worker burst into jeering laughter.

His heart metaphorically wilted, dried, and blew away into the unforgiving breeze as he listened to this most perfect creation speak about how she had manipulated him into buying her lavish gifts. The trio continued their deriding guffawing as they each called him names like "dope," "oaf," and… "flower girl." He listened to her say through her mocking laughter how he had a face that nobody could love. Probably not even his own mother. He then heard the male co-worker ask his love out for a date. Her response was an enthusiastic 'yes,' complete with an invitation back to her home after their dinner and movie.

Herbert wrote a note that said that he wasn't feeling well and that he was going home early for the day. As he exited the building, he looked down on the trash can that sat beside the exit door. There he found his bouquet of flowers that he had lovingly selected just for her. Just for this moment. They were just lying there, sadly mixed in with various papers, wrappers, cans, and bottles. They were crumpled and covered in cigarette butts, partially-eaten sandwiches, a banana peel, and sticky residue from discarded soda bottles.

What was to be the happiest day of his life had turned into the darkest. He went home and immediately went to his garden. He wept as he selected a new bouquet to give to his former love.

The following morning, he was greeted with an enthusiastic smile and light kiss on the cheek from her. He handed her coffee to her and presented her with his new bouquet. It did not escape him that she failed to inquire as to how he was feeling. He asked her to have a drink of the coffee, then breathe deeply the flowers' aroma. She did so, unsuspectingly. He explained to her how different plants and flowers have different effects upon people. He explained how the *combination* of certain flowers and plants, including coffee beans, can impact people. He explained how *some* of those impacts could result in the death of a person.

The young woman's eyes knowingly widened at his latest revelation. He watched as she began coughing. He watched as she began foaming at the mouth. He watched as her body began twitching. He watched as her eyes rolled back into her head. And he watched as her body slumped to the floor as she let out her final exhalation. His face held a solemn expression as he drank from her coffee cup and breathed deeply from her bouquet.

He looked down upon his lifeless, pathetic body before ascending further. He saw brilliant lights, then clouds, then silhouettes. They were dark silhouettes that did not become brighter as they approached. They remained black as they explained to him that he was not welcome in the Enlightenment. He had done an evil thing and he would not be allowed to ascend to the peace that is Enlightenment until he redeemed himself. He must right an evil, demonic wrong on the earth. Then and only then would he be considered for acceptance in Enlightenment. The dark forms then grabbed him and forced him to descend rapidly back to his body which was now placed in the city morgue.

And that is where Herbert Jenkins, the Botanist, has remained since 1952, Mrs. Roper concluded. *He has sat quietly in the corners of this morgue lamenting his lost love while looking over the various plants that are placed here. He rarely speaks to anyone. He does not believe in redemption for himself or for any other person. He believes that humans, including himself, are irredeemable and that he must suffer for all of eternity for what he has done.*

As Arima had been listening to Mrs. Roper's story, she had noticed that all of the plants that adorned the morgue's window sills had steadily begun to droop and wilt. She shook her head and wiped a tear from her eye before saying, "Wow, Herbert…or 'Mr. Botanist'…or whatever. That really sucks. I'm sorry that you went through all that. And I'm sorry for that woman, too. I mean, she sounds like she was a bitch, but she didn't deserve to die. Not for that. I mean, grow up. We all get a broken heart. Tell the bitch off and find someone new, but don't poison her! Sorry, but that's how I feel. Listen, I know you were treated badly by a lot of people, especially women, but we're not *all* bad. Hell, not even *most* of us are bad. Most people are actually *good*. We sometimes just make bad decisions and do bad things. You just got stuck with some bitches who were immature and shit and that warped your view of women. And believe me, I know some women who feel the *same way* about men. It's all so stupid how we prejudge people based on gender or anything else for that matter. But I'm telling you. We are *not* all bad! And that little girl wasn't bad. She didn't deserve to be raped and murdered. I don't know if helping me will get you to Enlightenment or not, but you sure as hell will take some sick bastards off the street and keep them from hurting others. C'mon, Herbert. I need you. That innocent girl's soul needs you. Please, help me just this once, okay?"

All of the plants on the windowsill began returning to their lush green hue. Their stems stood upright until they looked like a battalion of little soldiers waiting for their marching orders. In the middle of all of them, a large purple iris exploded into full bloom. Arima had her answer.

Chapter 8

Death by Bouquet

"Well, good morning sweetie," a beaming Jamie stated as she fluttered into the living room to greet her best friend. "How was your first night at work?"

"Uh…yeah…It was…um," Arima began as she searched for the proper words to use to describe her rather eventful first night at the morgue. She had fallen in love, communicated with the dead, banished an evil soul into a Workplace Harassment poster, and formed an alliance with another lost soul to murder racists. The only word that she could come up with was, "interesting."

"I just wanna get baked and fall into bed," she said to Jamie as she observed what was happening with the television set.

In the place of their high-tech, high-definition streaming television, there was a nineteen-inch black and white console that her other two housemates, Jessie and Cliff, were feverishly working on.

"So…what are *you* guys doing?" Arima inquired drowsily.

Cliff replied in a frustrated tone, "We're trying to get this damned dinosaur hooked up. One of the local TV stations has begun broadcasting from their old tower. But you have to have an old-fashioned TV set with an antenna. Right now, besides the radio or having a phone modem on your computer, this is the only way to get information. We found this old thing up in the attic and…"

At that moment, the television set began humming with black and white horizontal lines rolling on the screen. Cliff turned the channel knob until it rested on the appropriate number. He adjusted the antenna, and the rolling lines and static became a somewhat clear picture of a broadcaster, who was saying...

Again, ladies and gentlemen of our viewing audience, the wireless internet service throughout the world has been taken down by terrorists. The moment that it is repaired anywhere, it is overloaded and taken down again in about five minutes. Authorities and technicians are baffled by what might be the cause. In the meantime, the only way to get internet service is through old fashioned modems, if you happen to live in an area with phone lines, which is, of course, quite rare. And television streaming services are disabled as well. The management at this station is committed to bringing you the most up to date information and quality entertainment and that is why we have redeployed our broadcast tower. So tell your friends and neighbors to dust off their old antennae TV's and enjoy our programming until such time as this crisis is over. This news update has been brought to you by Sniffles *facial tissue. Wipe away your sniffles with* Sniffles. *Now, please enjoy this twelve-hour* Matlock *marathon. We will break in as the situation warrants.*

Jessie West stood in front of the television in morbid silence. Her lower lip began puckering and trembling. She then let out a tortured wail and ran into her bedroom in despair while screaming, "*Matlock?* What the hell is *Matlock?* My world has just ended! My online world that I have carefully cultivated! My online world where people can see me as I *want* them to see me! Now what am I supposed to do? Be *myself?* Who in the hell would ever be interested in the *real* me?"

Cliff hastily followed his wife as he tried to reassure her. "C'mon, baby, it'll be okay. *I* love the real you and other people will too. And…um…maybe we'll like *Matlock*. And Ooo! Ooo! I think they're playing *Car 54, Where Are You?* later. I think that I've heard of that. It'll all be okay baby. Please don't cry anymore."

"Wow," Arima replied flatly. "Now I *really* gotta get baked and then…"

No Arima, the Botanist's voice said to Arima's soul. *Please do not do that. I need to concentrate to complete my work and I'll be unable to do that if we are high. Please, just go to bed and go to sleep. I will take control of your body and do what needs to be done. All that I need to know is whether you want these men to die peacefully or…painfully.*

Arima thought back at the sadistic scene that she had witnessed of the dear child being brutally raped and murdered by this scum and said forcefully, "Painfully. Definitely painfully".

"What's that, sweetie?" Jamie inquired. "Did you say 'painfully?'"

"Oh…uh, yeah. Sorry," Arima replied as she thought, *I've gotta remember not to talk to these spirits out loud, dammit!* "I was just saying that this is definitely painful for poor Jessie. She's so wrapped up in her online personality, y'know? Anyway, I think I'll skip the hit. I'm just too tired. I'll see you later this evening before work."

"All right, dearie, nighty night!" Jamie cheerfully responded. "I've gotta go out for a bit, anyway, and show a house to a lovely couple. Now, where did I put my tape? My pantsuit for today is a bit…revealing in all the wrong areas, and I don't know how this cute little suburban family might…um…react. So many macho men out there who would just *die* to have a ten-inch penis and for me, it is a curse. Ah, well, nothing that my trusty tape can't handle."

Arima changed into her shorts and T-shirt, threw her work clothes on the floor of her closet, crashed face first onto her bed, and immediately fell into a deep slumber.

Seemingly five minutes later, Arima woke up. She wiped the sleep from her eyes and looked around. The sun was beginning to set outside of a filthy and cracked window. She was fully dressed and sitting on a stained and torn couch with a floral print. Sitting in front of her were two men who were wearing brown shirts and worn blue jeans with very visible urine stains. They had neo-Nazi tattoos and shaved heads. And they were bound by duct tape on two beat-up living room wooden chairs. They were the men that she had been shown. They were the last two murderers of that little girl.

They were struggling in vain to free themselves while saying, "Wh-wh-what the fuck, bitch? What the hell did you do to us? Let us go and maybe we won't kill you, you little bitch whore!"

Arima responded to the suffering pair with a simple, "Um…I don't know. I don't know *what* I have done to you".

It's all right, Arima, the Botanist said softly to her. *I'll explain it. Just let me regain control over your body and I will explain everything to these horrible men… and to you.*

"Um…all right, I'm pretty curious myself," Arima dryly replied out loud before her voice changed in its cadence slightly and the Botanist began explaining what he had done while in control of Arima's body.

"Well, you see, boys, I saw what you and your horrible friend did to that little girl. And we decided that you should not go on living so that you can do that to others. And once you die, Arima will take your souls and place them somewhere where you can never harm another person. Here is what I did. I went back to my old home and found the remnants of my beloved plants in the back yard. It was so sad to see my lovely garden in such a weed-infested state. Just as it is so sad to see how human weeds have infested our beautiful planet. I took the certain flowers that I needed for this and developed two different toxins."

"The first toxin I put into your sodas as you were gawking at and cat calling a woman at the convenience store. You called me such horrible names when I walked into the store. You whispered to me what you would do to me after I left the store. But by the time I found you outside waiting for me, you had already guzzled your sodas and you were both too woozy to care about me, so you went right to this hellhole of a home and you fell asleep."

"I followed you here and once you were asleep, I came in and obviously bound you to these chairs. *I* then waited for *you*. I waited for you to wake up so that I could tell you what *I* would do to *you*. What I would do to two spineless worms who get thrills by dominating others. Raping others. Murdering others. And all because they don't *look* like you or *love* like you or *believe* like you. You are all so sad and pathetic. I never thought much about humankind while I was alive, but I have learned that there are many good people out there. It's just that the *truly evil* people get all of the attention. You hear about such vile people over and over again until you get beaten down by it and you think horrible thoughts about everybody that you encounter. Instead of trusting others and believing in the goodness of others, you are always suspicious of others. You are always on the defense. What did that smile mean? Do they truly mean those words of support for me or are they just playing a cruel game? Do they truly like me or is it all just a manipulation? It all grows so tiresome. And we can *all* be cruel in our own ways. None of us are perfect. But most people's cruelty is unintentional. It is something that is said in the heat of the moment or something you do when you aren't thinking straight. It is cruelty that arises from an error in judgement. And then, the person feels remorse for their actions and tries not to repeat those hurtful actions.

"That is not true in your case. In your case, you *purposefully* hurt people. Your cruelty is *planned*. It is *calculated*. And it is acted upon with an unholy ferocity without any remorse. Without any sense of guilt or responsibility. *You* are the weeds that are infesting our beautiful garden. And in order for a garden to grow...to thrive...to reach its full beauty...well...the weeds must be pulled and discarded. Over and over and over. We must be ever vigilant in pulling the weeds. Otherwise, the constantly invading and growing weeds will take over and the garden will die. And the weeds will hold dominion over a dark and barren land that holds joy for no one.

"So it is now my duty...and my pleasure...to pull *these* weeds. To discard *you* so that you may never harm another soul ever again. You will want to hold your breath now."

Arima's spirit-controlled body got up from the beaten couch and picked up a beautiful bouquet of exotic flowers. Her body went up to the first bound man, grabbed him by the back of his head and thrust his face into the bouquet.

"Yes. Let's just see how long you can hold your breath before having to breathe deeply of my most deadly friends," the Botanist said through Arima's voice. The man's body shook as he attempted to hold his breath before finally succumbing and deeply breathing in the intoxicating fragrance of the flowers.

Arima's body then went to the second bound man and repeated the grave procedure. Her body sat back down on the beaten couch and waited.

"You see," the Botanist stated through Arima's voice. "What you have just inhaled is a quite potent combination of oils. The effect will be that the oils will combine in your system and begin attacking your internal organs. They will be ripped apart and will be torn from your body. It is an old Laotian recipe that I found a very long time ago. The most common forms of this toxin are as a lotion or a gas, but I found a way to combine the oils and scents of the plants themselves in a lovely bouquet to have the very same effect. It is really quite effective and really quite painful, as you are about to find out."

The men began violently convulsing. Their eyes rolled back into their heads and frothing blood mixed with saliva began drooling from their trembling mouths, oozing down the swastikas on their necks. They screamed in unholy agony as their brown shirts turned crimson. Their internal organs lumbered out of their torn abdomens and haphazardly fell to the floor with a discernible "plopping" sound.

Ah, very good, the Botanist said to Arima. *The weeds have been pulled from this earth. It is now up to you, Arima, to discard them for all time. To destroy their spirits so that they may never harm another in this or any other life again.*

"Uh, okay," a bewildered Arima replied. "Wow. That was really pretty cool. Okay, assholes, come on in. I'm taking you for a ride!"

Arima opened her soul once again and pulled the dark spirits into her essence. The Botanist then entwined the two vile souls in his spiritual vines of his own creation. The moment they began to speak, he covered their unearthly mouths tightly with his conjured leaves.

Arima left the shack and proceeded immediately to the morgue. She could feel the dark souls struggling to free themselves within her. As she was sneaking past the morgue toward the meeting room, she observed Marcus gazing in delight at an old magazine that was most certainly not intended for children…or some adults, for that matter. She chuckled to herself at the sight, then let out a boisterous internal laugh as The Botanist released his grip on the dark spirits and she expelled them into the Workplace Harassment poster.

She took the poster down, rolled it up to the muffled cries of the three entrapped demonic souls and went out the back exit. In the back alley, she placed the rolled-up poster into a burn barrel. She first lit a joint and inhaled with deep satisfaction. She then lit the poster. She did not know *how* she knew, but she knew that she could destroy these sadistic spirits if she destroyed the inanimate object that they had been trapped in. She watched with both sorrow and glee as the fire consumed the poster. She heard the anguished wails of the destroyed spirits float away with the spent ashes on the warm evening breeze.

Arima, I must leave you now, the Botanist said with slight regret. *I am being called to Enlightenment. I have redeemed myself. It has been a pleasure to get to know you. Thank you. Thank you for helping me move on. Perhaps now, I can find peace. But, before I go, let me tell you a little trick as to how to grow the most lovely marijuana plants. It will be like inhaling the nectar of the gods.*

As the Botanist whispered his secret into Arima's soul, she smiled more broadly than she had in her entire life.

Herbert Jenkins felt himself being lifted from Arima's body. He continued his ascension beyond the clouds until coming to a rest. He felt at peace and was surrounded by bright white light and a delicate mist. A silhouette approached him. It was dark at first, then became bright green as it came closer. Herbert once again looked upon the loveliest face he had ever seen. He had not fallen in love with her so many years ago just because of her physical beauty. He had also fallen in love with her name. It was her name that convinced him that they were meant to be together for all eternity.

"Hello, Herbert," the angelic green mouth stated.

"Um...hello, Iris Rose," Herbert bashfully replied. "It's been so long and...I am so sorry. I am so sorry for what I did to you. You did not deserve that. I wish that I could make it up to you."

"But you have, Herbert," Iris responded. "You *have* made it up to me. You have vanquished two demonic souls of Vetis. You have reduced his army. You have redeemed yourself. To me. And to the universe. And *I* am sorry for how I treated *you*. How I used you. And it wasn't just you. I manipulated many men in my time on earth. I certainly didn't deserve to be murdered for it, but it wasn't exactly nice of me. In fact, it was cruel. Because of how I died, I was allowed to join Enlightenment. But my punishment for all time is that I will forever be green. Green to match my jealous soul. That is why I manipulated men into buying me things. I was horribly jealous of others who had more than me. And that jealousy consumed me and compelled me to do cruel things. I was also made green by the powers of Enlightenment as a constant reminder of what I did to *you* and how I bastardized the love you had for your precious plants and flowers. I will always regret that, Herbert. And, I will always regret having to look this way."

A spiritual tear formed in Herbert's eye as he looked upon Iris and said, "You should never regret that. You are the most beautiful vision that I have ever seen in my life...or afterlife. To me, you are once again perfect."

"Come, then, Herbert," Iris sighed as she took his hand. "In Enlightenment, we can create our own world. We can surround ourselves with what makes us most happy. And I have used that ability to create something for *you*...for *us*." The mist lifted and they were standing in the middle of the most luxuriously beautiful garden. There was every type of plant from throughout the earth, and other worlds as well. The explosive array of scents, textures, and colors was overwhelming. For the first time in his existence, Herbert cried out with genuine rapture.

The spiritual form of a twelve-year-old Black girl emerged from a nearby forest and walked steadily toward the pair. Herbert looked down upon her with hopeful anticipation as the child said, "Thank you, sir. Thank you for avenging me. Thank you for ridding the world of those bad men. I can now rest peacefully here."

Tears once again began to form in Herbert's eyes as he said, "W-Would you like to rest peacefully *here*? With *us*? Would you like to join our family?"

The girl looked up at the couple and burst into tears as Herbert lifted her up. The new family embraced tightly as tears of peaceful joy poured out of their souls. The torrent of tears poured out of Enlightenment. The torrent of tears cascaded down towards the earth.

As an exhausted Arima was walking home, she was suddenly drenched by a downpour of warm rain. She looked up at the sky and instinctively understood that she was not being covered in rainfall. She smiled as she realized that she was being covered in the euphoria of a peaceful spirit.

Chapter 9

Today's Sermon

Sweat was flying off of the seventy-one-year-old Pastor's flailing forearms, forehead, and hair as he reached into his soul and delivered his rapturous Sunday morning sermon to his noticeably dwindling congregation. His veins protruded from his neck and his face was bright purple as he barked out with an uproarious cadence the various scriptures that were meticulously selected for this week's lesson for his entranced congregation.

He passionately preached repeatedly about the kindness of Jesus Christ. His charity. His mercy. His sacrifice. The parishioners wept. They rejoiced. They threw their hands up into the air and screamed "Hallelujah" or "Amen" precisely on cue. The sermon was an overwhelming success for those in attendance.

It was successful in the further entrenchment of these pliable souls into the work of Vetis, the Tempter of the Holy. It was successful in twisting the kindness, generosity, and selflessness of the preaching of Jesus Christ into a self-serving hatred of the other. The other that did not look like them. The other that did not love like them. The other that did not vote like them. The other who was indoctrinating their children into sinful thoughts and deeds through their "woke" schools and libraries. The other who was taking their country away from them through nefarious means. The other who sacrificed babies to their demonic beliefs in the basement of a pizza parlor. The other who was their sworn enemy. The other who they must *vanquish* in order to reclaim *their* rightful dominion over this country and this earth.

Such fools, the Pastor would chuckle to himself as he witnessed the joyfully ignorant acceptance on his flock's faces. *They have no idea that we are the other. I am the other. I am the one who is indoctrinating them. I am the one who is taking their freedom away. I am the one who is leading them to an existence of subservience to our great Vetis. They will be subservient upon this earth, and they will be subservient in the after life once we have gathered enough of their dark souls to conquer Enlightenment. The earth shall be ours. The heavens will be ours! And these fools will be the willful participants of their own demise. And I shall be one of the chosen few to sit at the side of Vetis and witness this most glorious oppression.*

The Pastor was still wiping his brow with a saturated handkerchief as he flashed his serpentine smile and shook the hands of his departing congregation. The final woman's hands were still shaking in rapturous excitement as she took the Pastor's disfigured hands into hers and looked at them. "Pastor," she softly inquired. "How is it that your hands are so broken?"

The Pastor's expression grew dark as he replied remorsefully, "My hands. My hands, and my body were beaten mercilessly by one of the unholy ones in 2003. He was such a brutal, godless soul. But by God's mercy, he is no longer upon this earth with us. But there are others just like him my child. Others who would harm you and your children in the same manner."

The woman looked up into the Pastor's black eyes and said with a soft determination, "We must kill them all, Pastor. We must or else they will kill us."

"Yes, my child," the Pastor sneered in response. "We must. And it will be your time to be called to action soon. Thank you, my child. Thank you for your loyalty and…servitude. Peace be with you. God be with you."

He watched with arrogance as his flock proceeded to their vehicles, many still adorned with flags and banners celebrating Vetis's failed attempt at permanently installing one of his many dullard "Golden Calves" into the most prominent political position in the world. As he looked upon the faded, tattered, and nearly twenty-year old symbols of hatred, ignorance, and blind subservience flapping in the cool morning breeze, his own arrogance began to fade and tatter as well.

The waving symbols had represented their best chance to usher in the

Age of Vetis. As a young man who was being groomed to be an earthly leader in the army of Vetis, he had been told of the ascension of an easily manipulated, narcissistic man who appeared charismatic to *other* easily manipulated and narcissistic people. Despite his diminished mental faculties, this man would hold the power to use his temperament, humor, and contrived conviction to tap into some people's fears and indoctrinate them into a cult of personality of hating anyone that was different from them and anything that they were not brainwashed to believe. Lies became truth and truth became "alternate facts" that would be quickly discarded by the logic- and informationally- impaired. They would be directed to march and dutifully shout simplistic three-syllable phrases. They would intimidate. They would bully. They would hate. This hatred would result in increasingly violent attacks upon civil society's most essential institutions of science, education and government. And this man *did* ascend to this most prestigious platform of power.

But not *permanently* as had been prognosticated. Pro-democracy forces battled this cult of usurpers at the election booth, airwaves, and neighborhoods that became literal battlefields. The autocratic movement of Vetis would strengthen and gain power in areas, only to be beaten back and fragmented once again. And now, in the year 2034, these freedom-fighters had apparently been successful in eliminating their most powerful tool to spread their deplorable lies and propaganda of insurgency: the wireless Internet.

As he watched the forces of his unholy movement become further degraded, he wondered if he would ever see the domination of Earth by Vetis in his lifetime. And if Earth was not conquered...if there could not be enough holy souls plunged into the blackness of their movement...then the conquest over Enlightenment would not be possible.

The Pastor had been placed upon this earth to recruit and indoctrinate others into the movement. He was one of many who would use people's fears to twist and bastardize their otherwise pure religious beliefs. It was from hundreds, if not thousands, of pulpits throughout the world that the earthly army of Vetis would be primarily built. His mission was to convince his unsuspecting sheep that they were doing the work of God, when in fact, they were doing the work of a power-hungry demon.

The Pastor mused to himself at how successful he had been in converting these otherwise kind people to wage war against others that they were *told* to wage war against. He thought about the hundreds of names that had been sent into battle. He laughed out loud as he thought about the hundreds of his followers whose blood had been shed and whose dark souls were now congregating in the netherworld, awaiting their orders to attack Enlightenment. He had been so successful at this aspect of the plan.

And the plan was a quite simple one. Convert otherwise good people to hate others. Indoctrinate them into believing violence against the hated others was God's work. Expand their ranks and dominate the earth with brutal, autocratic regimes. Sacrifice them on the earth's battlefields and reconstruct them as an army of dark souls in the afterlife. Attack and conquer Enlightenment. And then, welcome the glorious arrival and eternal dominion of Vetis.

The Pastor felt his arrogance re-emerge as he thought about his earthly manipulative victories. But his arrogance was once again short-lived as he witnessed the ceiling, floor, and walls of his modest church become encased in a thick, dark purple smog. And his heart sank as he heard an all-too-familiar, snide, nasally voice penetrate his very essence.

My, aren't we full of ourselves this morning, the sinister apparition stated as its tightly bound copper hair emerged from behind the pulpit and rose to full prominence through the dense purple fog. *I have been listening to your thoughts, Pastor. And yes, you have been quite successful in manipulating the weak into the service of our most glorious Vetis. But you have failed miserably at your most important commission.*

You have failed to produce a daughter with extraordinary power to fight and serve alongside us. It was through this daughter that we would have our most powerful ally. You failed in seducing your daughter to cower to our whims. You failed in seducing our *daughter. And now, she has become one of the leading forces against our movement. Instead of recruiting her, you have turned her into our sworn enemy. And she is powerful. She is dangerous. And she must be eliminated.*

"Me? What about you?" The Pastor yelled back incredulously. "*I* wasn't the one who allowed your husband's family to groom her. *I* wasn't the one who allowed those interlopers to give her a sense of righteous conviction and self-worth! She wasn't even biologically *related* to them and yet *they* succeeded at taking her from us! I tried to indoctrinate her. I tried to seduce her into our ways by any means necessary including sexual domination! And what did I get for it? Her bastard uncle beat me! Disfigured me for life! That is why I left Madison all those years ago and came to Louisiana. Our daughter was and still is a lost cause. But I have another daughter now. She just turned twenty-three and..."

The Pastor was abruptly interrupted by the ghastly spirit. *...And she has just become aware of her powers. Yes, I am quite aware of your Arima. I am quite aware at her ability to connect with and absorb the souls of those who are trapped here and unable to enter Enlightenment. I am quite aware of her ability to imprison those souls in inanimate objects and destroy them forever through the destruction of those inanimate objects. I am well aware of her great gift. And I am well aware at what an asset she could be for us...if you are able to re-enter her life and convince her to join you. But, she has too much of her mother and her grandmother in her. She must be indoctrinated, Pastor. With brutal force if necessary.*

I am also quite aware at just how dangerous she could be to us and our glorious movement. She must be convinced, or she must be destroyed. Just as I will personally destroy that little whore of a daughter that we darkened this earth with. I will take care of our daughter, and our granddaughter. I just need to find a soul who hates that little bitch as much as I do. Then, I will be able to entwine my soul with theirs and murder our little bundle of joy and her damned offspring! Yes, that little bitch is a lost cause as well. All peace and love with no thirst for violence or domination over others. But she could be dangerous as well. If she is able to tap into the attributes that she possesses from her whore mother and her damned father, then she could also be quite formidable. So my granddaughter must be sacrificed as well. And I will laugh as my husband and his family weep as they watch their beloved succumb to my icy grip of death.

But I am now warning you, just as I have already warned Arima. She must not become involved with our daughter. She must stay away from New York. I have spooked her and her grandmother enough, I believe, that it shouldn't be a problem. They aren't aware that I pose no real threat to them...yet.

Once I kill our daughter, she will not be allowed into Enlightenment. Not with all of the vengeful acts that she has committed in her forty-six years. Her soul will be trapped here. And the only being that will be able to make contact with her and allow her to re-emerge as a threat to us once again will be Arima. Your daughter. Our daughter's half-sister. If the two of them are allowed to join forces, either on Earth or in the spirit world, I fear that our dream of domination by our most glorious Vetis shall be vanquished. Yes, Pastor, consider that. As a unified force, they will be that powerful. They and their followers will have the power to defeat us.

So, Pastor...I'll take care of our *little mistake. You are to convert Arima. And, if you fail once again to bring one of your offspring into our fold, then you must do to her what you did to her mother. You must kill her. You must slice her open on a sacrificial altar. You must behead her and put her head on a spike as a tribute to our glorious Vetis. Do you understand?*

"Of course I understand!" The Pastor roared back. "I have no feelings for that girl. She is no more important to me than any of these other lemmings that we recruit to do our bidding. Except, in her case, she is quite powerful. And despite her upbringing by her damned Grandmother, she still has a part of *me* in her as well. She has an ember of domination burning in her that I *will* exploit. I *will* succeed this time. And if I do not...then...Arima will die at my tortured hands."

Yes, she has a part of you in her. But may I remind you that our *daughter was made up of* both *of us and look at the disaster that she has become. I could almost sense it when she was growing in my womb. The way she would violently kick me. And once she was born and rejected my mother's milk, I instinctively knew that she was not destined to join us. As she grew from infant to toddler to child to young woman, she always had a rebellious streak against anything that did not seem right to her. I thought that I could beat her rebelliousness out of her. Perhaps I could have, if left alone, but I could only go so far with my husband's family watching over us. They were quite dangerous. But I don't really need to tell* you *that, now do I?*

I, too, was arrogant. I believed that I, along with the pathetic excuse of a man who thought he was her father, could mold her and brutally bend her to our will. But the more I beat her, the stronger she became. The more spiteful that little bitch became. That is when I sent her to you. To her true father. I believed that with my beating her body and soul and you raping her body and soul, that she would eventually succumb. That she would fall in line. And then, in her weakened state, we could rebuild her in our image. But it was never to be. My arrogance blinded me to the truth that she was a bad seed that should have been aborted. I had planned on doing just that when she was fifteen. I was planning on finally aborting that unwanted burden, but you *convinced me to just let her go. You said that my husband's damned family finally had a complete grip on her and that they would destroy us if we harmed her. Perhaps you were right, but now look at the threat that she has grown into.*

So do not depend too much on your genetic influence, Pastor. Genetics can only go so far against a person that holds true conviction and compassion for others of their kind. The question is...does Arima have any conviction towards anything or anyone besides her own selfish gratification? Because if not, you may have a chance at bringing her into our army. But if she is anything like her half-sister, then...we shall proceed without her.

Chapter 10

Youthful Indiscretions

"Awwww, yeah, man...this is the best pizza ever," a satisfied Arima stated hazily as she took the last bite of the last slice of pizza.

"Arima...what the hell!" Jessie exclaimed as she, her husband, Cliff, and fellow housemate Jamie entered the room with their drinks. "You ate the whole damn pizza? And you didn't even *pay* for it! I swear, you can be the most *selfish* person in the world!"

Cliff and Jamie could do nothing more than chuckle as Arima replied through her intoxicated haze, "Oh...hey, man...I'm sorry...but it's like...this is the best pizza ever. I just couldn't stop. Hey, are there any more of those cookies that you baked yesterday? Those were the best cookies ever."

"No," Jessie tersely replied with her arms folded and a look of disgust on her face. "No, you ate all of those yesterday while we were at work."

"Ahhhh, shit...Yeah," Arima replied. "How 'bout potato chips? We have some, right?"

Jessie sat next to her friend, took her hand and looked at her seriously. "Arima, we have been the best of friends since high school, and I love you. I truly do. You're totally chill and you are probably the least judgmental person that I know. You're fun to party with and have a great sense of humor. You are the greatest confidant and never spread gossip...probably because you don't remember any, but it's still a good quality. You are a fantastic person, and I am so grateful that you are in my life, but I want you to listen to me now."

Jessie's tone then immediately changed from irreverence to a roar. "When you are high, you are a damned pig! You eat *everything* in the house! You don't just get the munchies. You get the munchies on *steroids*! You are *literally* eating us out of house and home! So get off your ass and go to the grocery store! You've already eaten everything that Cliff and I have bought this week and it's not Jamie's turn yet. So, get up and get us some food!"

"Wait…what…now?" a confused Arima replied.

"Yes, now!" Jessie answered through her grinding teeth. "While you're gone, we'll just order another…oh never mind. I'm not telling you. You'll hide in the bushes and hijack it. Please, Arima. Just go and get us some food."

"Fine, I could use the exercise anyway," Arima replied in an uninterested tone as she got off of the couch, scratched her ass, brushed pizza crumbs from her top and put her jacket on over her pajamas.

An hour and a half later, Arima's three housemates were basking in the glow of post-pizza consumption.

"Wow," Jamie stated. "Arima was right. That may be the best pizza ever. And I'm not even high right now. That was almost better than sex."

"Almost?" Cliff chimed in. "That was *definitely* better than…"

Cliff thought it wise to not finish his statement once he saw his wife's brilliant blue eyes dart at him.

Arima entered the home, carrying two large grocery bags. "All right, here ya go. Can you guys put this stuff away for me? I gotta go see Grams before my shift tonight and I'm running a little late. I kinda got hung up at the store. Why are there so many types of cookies? I mean, there are so many, and they all look so good."

"Yeah, we can do that, sweetie," a chuckling Jamie replied as she took the bags from her friend and the trio entered the kitchen as Arima made her way up the stairs to get ready for work.

"Okay, we're not sending her to the store high *ever again*! I mean, how the hell did she eat three frozen burritos?" Jessie cried out as she looked at the contents of the grocery bags. There were three frozen burrito wrappers, a half-eaten bag of potato chips, an empty container of onion dip, a half-eaten box of peanut butter breakfast cereal, two candy bar wrappers, two empty packages of lemon cookies, and- for some unexplained reason- an onion.

Arima sauntered into her grandmother's home and announced her arrival. "Hey, Grams! I'm here! I brought you a 'nilla milkshake!"

Louise Azar came out of her kitchen in her flowing, brightly-colored robe and took the large paper cup from her beloved granddaughter. "Thank you, my child. That was so sweet of..."

Her thought trailed off as she realized that the milkshake was only about half-full. She shook her head, chuckled, and said, "Come, child, and tell me how your job is going. Have you had any...experiences?"

A now near-sober Arima relayed to her grandmother her violent exploits with the racists and The Botanist. Although Louise Azar had witnessed and participated in many incredible episodes in her life, she sat bewildered at the recounting of her granddaughter's adventures. She had sensed that Arima was powerful. But until this moment she had not realized just *how* powerful. She had not realized that Arima had the ability to completely control the spirits that she allowed into her soul. She had feared that a powerful dark soul might be able to consume and control her granddaughter, leaving Arima's body and soul helpless to defend herself against whatever the dark spirit may wish to do with it. This fear had now been mostly alleviated.

And she was apparently the first Azar woman who could permanently destroy the dark spirits that had been placed in inanimate objects through the destruction of those objects. Every Azar woman had tried to destroy Howard, whose darkened spirit was trapped in the beautiful painting of a Jamaican harbor. He, along with the painting, would be placed in a fireplace, or chopped to pieces with an axe or weighed down and drowned at the bottom of a lake.

It was all to no avail. The next morning, a completely restored painting would be hanging on the wall with evil chuckles emanating from it. They realized that the dark spirit had complete dominion over the object that it was imprisoned in. It could call upon its spiritual powers and restore these objects, thereby restoring their life in the afterlife. But they could not *leave* those objects. Not without being invited into the soul of someone such as

Arima. So all of the Azar women resigned themselves to simply being the guardian of these haunted artifacts and ensure that the spirits that were trapped there were not allowed to escape.

This was not true of Arima. She held dominion over both the evil souls *and* their inanimate prison. She could take them into herself. She could place them into objects. She could manipulate them. And she could extinguish their essence for all time. She could destroy them through the simple act of setting them on fire or smashing them into pieces as nonchalantly as she could crumple up a wad of paper.

Louise realized that she was a more evolved version of herself and their Azan descendants. That she was a stronger warrior against pure evil than any of them had ever been. Louise allowed herself a moment of relaxation as relief replaced her great anxiety.

The relief was short-lived, however. Louise immediately thought that, although her strength was a blessing, it could also be a curse. That her strength might give Arima a false sense of invincibility and that, in turn, may lead her into battles that she would not be and could not be prepared for. This false sense of invincibility might lead her back to her despised father or whoever the copperhead was. Louise realized that it was her responsibility to temper her granddaughter's confidence in her gifts.

"Well, that is quite interesting, dear," Louise began casually. "Yes, quite interesting indeed. It is nice to know that you have that ability over...shall we say...*lesser* demonic forces. I mean, these puny little racists that you destroyed are, *of course*, at the *lowest* rung of the ladder as far as power and influence goes. You would do well to remember that. You sensed it, didn't you? You were able to sense just how powerful they were, or in this case, weren't. You could sense that you could easily overpower them."

"And that is the precise ability that we are going to have you hone. You must trust your feelings. Your sensations. If you sense that a spirit is more powerful than you, then you must leave it alone. Do not trifle with it. Whatever battle they are engaged in is *not* your battle. Do not, *under any circumstances*, let them in. They will overpower you. They will control you. And they will *destroy* you. Do you understand, my child?"

"Uh...sure, Grams," Arima replied dismissively. "Hey, you got any cookies?"

"Arima!" Louise barked out.

"What? Jeezus!" a shocked Arima responded.

"Arima, my dearest," Louise began again as she took Arima's delicate hands in hers. "Please listen to me. Please take this seriously. I have seen things, Arima. I have done things. I have gone up against very powerful forces of evil. There was a time when I thought that I could control any evil spirit that I allowed in. I would take them in and imprison them in a painting, plate, or vase. I would do this as easily as you have just done. I became conditioned to believe that my powers were far greater than any evil in this universe. I became arrogant. And I was wrong. My arrogance nearly killed me.

"Let me tell you a story of a time when I was not much older than you. When I was twenty-five years old, I had quite a bit of experience with my… abilities. Your mother was about five at the time and I left her with my younger brother, who was seventeen, as I had a date with someone that I was quite attracted to. It was as though he held a spell over me, and I was drawn to him. It was a magical evening until…he raped and nearly murdered me.

"As he was on top of me and strangling me, I was able to reach around, and I grabbed a large rock. I struck him fiercely in the head with it and he rolled off of me. I was enraged and struck him over and over with it until his head and face was bloody mush. It was then that I realized that it wasn't this young man who had done this to me. It may have been his body, but his body was being controlled by an evil spirit. I was so entranced by this young man and…well, I'm a bit ashamed to say…but I was a bit…aroused by him, so I ignored what my senses were telling me about him. I ignored the feelings of danger. I was so dismissive of it that I actually wondered to myself, *Why is it that good girls fall for bad boys?* Had I just left him alone and not gone out with him that night, this horrible event never would have happened. But my selfishness and libido overrode the danger that I was sensing. So, he raped and strangled me in the front yard of my home. And I, in turn, murdered that young man.

"Now you may be wondering how it was that this evil spirit came to control this young man. I was, and still am, involved in a group of women. We all have various skills and abilities, and we frequently meet to…well… that's another story for another time. Let's just say that we meet to look after our loved ones as best as our abilities will allow. There were three young women about my age in this group. I do not know why, but these three young women did not like me. Perhaps it was just petty jealousy or something more. Well…now that I think about it I did…how can I say this… steal one of their boyfriends away. So, this made this group of three best friends quite upset with me and they decided to eliminate me, which I felt was a bit of an overreaction on their part.

"One of the women had the same ability as us. She could absorb a soul into her or place it into an inanimate object, but nothing more. A second young woman possessed an amazing power. She was the only one that I have ever known. She had the power to control and manipulate energy, including that of souls. So she could take the energy of the soul that had been captured by the first woman and place it into another human being. And the third woman possessed the power of manipulating the spirit's actions. She could control the spirit that was controlling its human host.

"These three women found a human host in another town that they thought nobody would miss for a while. They found a spirit that was trapped here. They captured that spirit in the soul of one woman, then transferred that spirit's energy into the human host, then controlled the actions of that human host. And that human host that was being controlled by an evil spirit that was being controlled with the most vengeful of the women, seduced me.

"As I said, the moment I killed that young man, I knew that he had been possessed, because I saw and felt the evil spirit billow out of him, like some grey cloud of smog. At that very moment, my brother came running outside to see what was happening. The first woman absorbed the dark soul. The second woman transferred that soul's energy into my brother's body. And the third woman had that dark soul that was inhabiting my brother attack me. My brother's body lunged at me, and I reacted instinctively. I picked up a large log and struck him with it. He fell backward and he was impaled on the picket fence that surrounded our lovely flower garden in our front yard. Those three harlots took off into the night and the evil spirit left my brother's body and floated away as I stood there and watched my dear brother die. His blood was dripping down the wooden fence posts as he was gasping for air. He looked up at me and extended his hand. I was, of course, crying profusely and screaming how sorry I was. In his last breath, he said to me, *It's okay. It wasn't your fault. I love you and I will always be with you.* And he has been from that day forward."

Louise wiped a tear from her eye, got up from her sofa and stood in front of a scenic painting of three palm trees swaying in the breeze. She smiled briefly before continuing. "Now, those three women disappeared and hid from me. But another woman in our group had the ability to track down specific souls and she told me where they were. So, one by one, I snuck into the houses that they were hiding in, and I slit their throats. They, of course, were not allowed entry into Enlightenment upon their deaths, so I absorbed their souls and placed them into a painting. This painting. And now, my dearest Arima, I believe that I am tired of looking at this painting. Would you do your ol' Grams a favor and place it in the fire for me?"

The palm trees in the painting immediately wilted and three dark silhouettes began flying through the brush strokes in a frenzy as they pleaded with Louise and Arima for mercy. Their screams reached a fevered pitch as Arima threw the painting into the fire. The flames licked around the edges, then burst through the center and the women's dark souls were put to their final end in the ashes of oblivion.

Heh, heh, heh, you bitches are toast! Arima heard a sinister voice say from the painting on the opposite wall.

"Shut up, Howard or you're next," came Arima's terse reply. The painting did not make another sound.

As Louise and Arima watched the final flames recede from the wooden embers in the fireplace, Louise put her arm around Arima's shoulder and whispered into her ear, "My point of this story, my dear child, is trust your instincts. *Always* trust your instincts." A bewildered Arima could do nothing more than give a silent nod of understanding.

Chapter 11

Freudian and Other Unfortunate Slips

"So," Marcus began as he was avoiding eye contact with Arima by shuffling papers that had already been organized. "I...uh...well...I noticed that you're not on the schedule tomorrow night."

"Uh...nope," Arima replied as she could feel her anticipation building. "I have the next two nights off. Why do you ask?"

"Well," Marcus answered reservedly as he continued to avoid looking directly at Arima. "I have tomorrow evening off, too, and...well...I was just thinkin' that since *I* was off and *you* were off then maybe...um...maybe we could get off together...I mean, do something together on our night off... y'know...if ya want to."

Arima fought back the urge to giggle at Marcus's obvious Freudian slip as her heart began pounding. "Uh, yeah...sure. I would *love* to hang with you. What did you have in mind?"

Marcus's mind was whirring as he tried to think of the appropriate response. He hadn't actually thought about any sort of plan. He just knew that since her hug alleviated all of his pain a few nights earlier, that he couldn't stop thinking about her. And he knew precisely what he wanted to do with her. But he also knew that that was way too forward of a suggestion at this moment. So he summoned up all of his courage, took a big gulp, and said coolly, "Eat?"

Arima couldn't hold it in any longer. His fumbling attempts at asking her out were just too cute, so she burst out in laughter. "Eat? Um...okay," she managed to reply through her chuckles. "You mean dinner? Sure. That would be great. And then maybe we could go back to my place and hang for a while...like...up in my room...if ya want".

"Sure, sure, sure," a nearly hyperventilating Marcus replied quickly. "Um...um...um, where would you like to go? You know...to eat?"

"I want you to take me to your favorite place," Arima replied coyly.

Following making the arrangements for their first date, a smiling Marcus left the morgue with a proud strut and Arima began joyfully bouncing on the balls of her black canvass tennis shoes while squealing in delight.

Well, Arima...it looks like you do *have a boyfriend*, came Mrs. Roper's playful voice.

Yes, Arima. Congratulations, Mr. Roper replied. *Marcus is a fine young man. We're very happy for you, but...*

"But what," a fearfully intrigued Arima asked of the bodiless voices.

Well, Arima, Mrs. Roper answered, *we just want to give you a bit of advice. We do not want you to repeat our mistakes. We haven't had a chance to tell you why we are trapped here and now that you have a love interest, we believe that the time is right. Isn't that right, dear?*

Yes, of course, Mr. Roper responded. *Arima, we have been here for fourteen years. Since the year 2020. We had been married for seven years and had two small children. Our daughter was five and our son was three at the time of our death. For the last two years of our marriage...well...when we were living...we were just horrible to one another. We had allowed ourselves to grow apart. We did not consider our two small children. We became selfish. We both began having affairs. When we weren't out looking to get laid at some neighborhood bar, we were spying on one another. Our jealousy continued to grow and the more jealous we became of one another, the crueler we were to one another. And our children would be sitting at home with some babysitter, while we were out cavorting. All they ever learned from us was that we either weren't home to attend to their needs or we were constantly fighting. We provided a horrible upbringing for them. We provided a horrible example of how to be parents. Hell, we provided a horrible example of how to be decent human beings.*

The night that we died; I had drunk way too much. I followed my wife and some man to a seedy hotel. I burst into the room and found them together. In a fit of jealous rage, I took the bottle of vodka that I had and crushed the man's head with it. I killed him. He hadn't really done anything wrong. Just a typical guy carousing the streets for a good time. We were the ones that were wrong. Our infidelity towards one another and my violence. I killed that man that night.

We both killed him that night, dear, Mrs. Roper replied in a supportively somber tone.

Yes, perhaps, but I swung the bottle. *He had a huge laceration from the top of his head to his throat. We just sat there and watched him bleed out. We were both drunk and in shock. We decided to leave and not tell anyone. And in my impaired state, I went the wrong way down a one-way street. I turned the corner and crashed headlong into an on-coming car. Both cars exploded. We were killed instantly.*

And those teenagers in the other car were killed instantly too, Mrs. Roper added. *Four sixteen-year-old kids out on a double date coming home from bowling, we understand. They did not deserve that. Our selfishness. Our infidelity. Our damned drunken jealousy killed five innocent people that night. And not only that, but it also destroyed our children.*

Yes, Mr. Roper continued. *They are now nineteen and seventeen. They went to live with my sister's family, and they have been wonderful to them. But they have had to live with the fact that their parents are murderers. They have been picked on and ridiculed. They both have such a hard time making friends. And despite my sister's and her husband's best efforts, it seems as though they are doomed to not understanding how to have healthy relationships. They are introverted and distrustful. And that is our fault. And we have been told that we must make that right with them before we are allowed entry into Enlightenment. We have waited fourteen years for someone like you to come along, Arima. Someone that we could connect with who could perhaps help us. Fourteen years we have had to think about how to make amends. And we don't have a clue as to what to do.*

So, Arima, Mrs. Roper began again, *the reason why we are telling you this is, just be kind to other people, especially those that you love. We understand that this is your first date, but that look in both of your eyes is unmistakable. You were both so delighted when you first saw one another. Don't ever lose that. Don't ever forget what it was you first saw in that other person. Don't become complacent and don't allow yourselves to take each other for granted. Just be kind to one another and remember what it was that first attracted you to that other person. What it was that made your heart flutter. If you do that, all of the silly little things are just that. They won't seem important to you. They will just be silly little things that just a bit of kindness and understanding and honest expression can take care of. That is all it takes. But if you allow those toxic feelings to build, then your relationship will go* down a dark path. And it will be your fault. Both of you. Just as it was our fault that we stopped communicating with one another. Stopped being thoughtful of one another. The end of your relationship may not hold the same deadly tragedy as our ending, but it will end tragically, nonetheless. Please take our advice Arima and cherish the love you have for this man and that he has for you. Because that type of love...that type of connection is hard to come by in this, or any, life.

And one other thing, Arima, Mr. Roper interjected. *We know this isn't your burden, but if you have any ideas as to how we can help our children and make up for the dastardly example that we set for them...well...we will always be in your debt.*

"Wow, um, yeah," a mournful Arima replied. "Wow. I'm so sorry, you guys. I'm sorry you did all that stuff and that those innocent people died. And I promise that I've listened to you. I'll try to be really cool to Marcus, even if he pisses me off. And I also promise that I will help you, somehow. I don't know how yet, but I'll think of something, or else my name isn't Arima Azan. And that's my name, so that's how it's going to be."

———

Arima arrived the following evening at seven o'clock at the address that Marcus had given her. Her heart leapt once again as she approached the dinery and saw him sitting outside waiting for her with tell-tale smoke tumbling from between his lips.

"Hey, uh...you want a drag?" Marcus offered as a greeting. "Oh, hell, yeah," Arima enthusiastically replied as she took the joint from his hand and savored the rich smoke coming from the spliff that had just been in her future lover's mouth. "This is, like...my favorite thing to do before coming here. This is *totally* my favorite restaurant, too! How 'bout we get it to go and go back to my place and put on a movie while we eat? I can dig out my old DVD's and find somethin' to watch."

Thirty minutes later, Arima sauntered through her front door with Marcus in tow. They were carrying seven take out bags. Jessie, Cliff, and Jamie looked up in amazement as Arima said to them without breaking her stride, "Everybody, this my friend Marcus. Marcus, this is everybody. We're goin' up to my room to...um...eat and stuff. We'll be down later...probably."

Arima gleefully jumped on the bed with both knees and began unpacking their treasure. Within moments, the pair were staring at a culinary smörgåsbord that consisted of eight double cheeseburgers, two large fries, four fruit pies, four twenty-piece chicken nuggets, fifteen dipping sauces of every variety, two large onion rings, two large chocolate milkshakes, four chicken sandwiches, two diet sodas and for some unexplained reason, a packet of apple slices.

The engorged pair laid in the bed following their gluttonous endeavor with wide smiles of satisfaction as the images of their selected horror movie DVD flickered on the television. The bed was littered with crumbs, globs of ketchup, colorful junk food wrappers, empty drink cups and one unopened packet of apple slices. Arima looked over at Marcus and began laughing.

"Wh-what's so funny?" a nearly exhausted Marcus asked.

"Oh, my God, you have a pickle stuck to your face!" Arima cried out, nearly wetting herself from the uncontrolled laughter.

Marcus then began laughing and retorted playfully, "Oh yeah? Well, I sure as hell hope that's ranch dressing on your lips!"

"Why don't you taste it to find out?" Arima asked provocatively as she gazed into Marcus's eyes.

Thirty minutes and one set of broken bedsprings later, the pair descended the staircase and entered the living room to the knowing snickers of Arima's three housemates.

"Oh, sweetie," Jamie scolded. "Go upstairs and change your shirt. You have ranch dressing all over it."

"What?" Arima replied casually. "Oh, uh…yeah. That's what it is. I'll be right back."

While Arima was upstairs hastily going through her laundry hamper to find a "clean" shirt, Marcus was looking at the floor, nervously shuffling his feet.

"Oh, sweetie," Jamie began in order to reduce the awkwardness of the situation. "We have heard sooo much about you and we are sooo happy to finally meet you. Our Arima has been talking about you night and day, and…"

Jamie was then cut off by Jessie who interrupted with, "Yeah, she talks about you a lot. I mean, when she isn't eating everything in the house, that is. And from the…er…sounds that just came from her bedroom, I guess you make her pretty happy. So join us, won't you? We're just watching…what the hell *are* we watching, anyway?"

Cliff answered meekly, "It's a marathon of something called *Cheers*. It's actually kind of funny Jess. I actually know quite a bit about this show. For example, did you know that…"

"Shut up. No, you don't know *anything* about this show. You're just making stuff up again. And, no, it's really not funny," Jessie interrupted with a snotty attitude. "None of this old crap is any good. There wasn't anything worth watching since before the reboot of the reboot of the reboot of *Real Wives* in 2030. And that, my friends, is a *fact*. Those shows like *Real Wives* is *reality*. It is how the world actually *is*. *These* old shows from the stone age are just made-up stories by writers. They are fake. Fake characters, fake plots, fake stories. Fake! *Real Wives* is real. It's in the title! I guess the next thing you're going to tell me is that this next show that's coming on is funny, too. What or who the hell is *Seinfeld*, anyway? I can't stand this anymore. I need some reality in my life. I'm just going to go into the bedroom and read the *Inquirer*. Nice to meet you, Marcus. C'mon, Cliff!"

"So, that's Jessie and Cliff," came Arima's voice as she re-entered the living room. "They've been together since high school. He was a big-time jock, and she was the head cheerleader."

"With an emphasis on the *head*," Jamie squealed out in delight.

"Shut up! I can hear you!" Jessie yelled out from behind her closed bedroom door, eliciting even greater childish laughter from Jamie and Arima.

"Sorry, sweetie! Couldn't resist! We won't talk about you anymore!" Jamie yelled out before huddling between Arima and Marcus and dropping her voice to a whisper. "Now, just between us, Jessie is a peach. She was the only popular girl and he was the only popular guy in high school who would befriend a stoner slacker like Arima and a burgeoning drag queen such as myself. So they truly are wonderful people. Of course, it didn't hurt that Arima and I helped them quite a bit with their homework, but still, we all became the unlikeliest best of friends. It's just that…well…Jessie is a bit… informationally challenged and Cliff is a bit…um…how should I say this?"

"Cliff has no balls, is completely pussy-whipped, and allows Jess to lead him around by his nose," Arima blurted out. "But Jamie's right. They are both very nice. Plus, being with them helps us get into clubs that we wouldn't ordinarily be allowed into, so there's that benefit."

"Oh! That reminds me!" Jamie screamed out. "There's an underground drag show tonight. Do you kiddies wanna go? I just hate going out by myself. We need all the eyes we can get to keep a lookout for the cops and the deplorables. *Pleeeease?*"

Arima looked at Marcus with quiet trepidation. This was his first test. He was so nice. Certainly he couldn't be one of the oppressive haters, could he? Certainly he wasn't a homophobe or transphobe, right?

Arima did not have to wait long for her answer, as Marcus jumped up from the couch, hastily made his way to the door, and exclaimed, "Hell, yeah! That sounds fun! What are we waiting for? Let's go!"

As the gleeful trio made their way down the street, a lurking figure appeared from out of the evening fog. He heard a nasally voice in his head say, *Ah, your daughter has a new boyfriend. That will be her Achilles' heel. Manipulate him to manipulate her. And if he does not go along, then threaten him. Threaten his life. Imprison him and force her to do our bidding. And once we have Arima in the fold, I will be able to focus on ridding ourselves of our whore of a daughter. And then, the games can truly begin.*

Chapter 12

The Foreplay is Now Over

*Drip...Drip...Drip...*was all that Marcus could hear from a nearby leaky faucet. The dreaded sound had become almost as torturous as the seemingly endless waterboarding that he had been forced to endure for the previous two days. He could smell the dankness of the room from underneath his black hood. Blood, saliva, tears, and snot were trailing down his beaten face and congealing just above his shattered collarbone. He wondered why this was happening. He wondered why he had been chosen to be a victim of this brutality.

His mind raced to find a happier place. A place where the pain could dissipate for just a moment and give his tortured body and soul a brief reprieve. He thought of Arima. For the past three months, he and Arima had been nearly inseparable. They spent every waking, non-working moment together. Holding hands during long strolls to the convenience store for chocolate donuts, potato chips, or slushies. Gazing longingly into one another's eyes as they shared a milkshake. Laughing together as they rolled on Arima's bed following blissful lovemaking. She was the person that had become his best friend. His lover. His soul mate.

And the unbridled happiness did not come just from his new love. He also felt a renewed energy and zeal for life as his cancer-riddled mother had actually received some good news about her prognosis. There was a new drug that, although not a cure, could substantially improve the quality and length of her life. His father was beyond himself with joy as he embraced his life-long love following the consultation with the physician. They wanted to share the good news with their new pastor and invited him over for a Saturday evening dinner.

The pastor was a tall, lanky, seventy-one-year-old white man. He entered the Jeffersons's home with a confident charisma. He greeted Marcus's parents and delicately kissed his mother on the forehead before embracing her. The pastor was new to their church. He was introduced six weeks earlier, following the sudden disappearance of their previous clergy. The previous pastor had been found in the swamp, half-eaten by alligators and other assorted wildlife. There was no explanation. But the new pastor attempted to shine a light on what may have happened to him.

He explained that there were evil, anti-Christian forces that were attempting to divide people by race. That was why most churches were now segregated. The Make America Godly Again, ultra-radical, white Christian nationalist people had grown distrustful, if not outwardly hostile, of non-white people. And, non-white people were increasingly fearful of white people, regardless of their societal views. That was why he assumed this position of looking over a nearly all-Black flock to go along with his responsibilities at an all-white church. He stated that he wanted to be a bridge between the two groups and heal the wounds that this senseless murder at the hands of white fascists had re-opened. And this joyous dinner to celebrate Mrs. Jefferson's good news was the perfect opportunity for people from two very different cultures to celebrate with one another. To rejoice with one another. To cry with one another. And to laugh with one another.

The pastor had been subtly encouraging Marcus to invite his girlfriend to his Sunday evening service. Arima had been quite resistant as she did not believe that she needed to be preached to in order to be a good person, but because it seemed so important to Marcus, she finally agreed to attend. And she did attend, the following morning. What the pastor had not considered, however, was that Marcus's girlfriend would also bring her grandmother along.

Arima's grandmother, Louise, absolutely adored Marcus. He was obviously in love with her cherished granddaughter, but there was more to it than that. She loved his carefree attitude while also being a young man that took his responsibilities seriously. She admired the sacrifices that he was making in order to support his parents through their difficulties. And she found him to be hysterically funny. She would look at her granddaughter gazing into the eyes of her new boyfriend and could sense that this was a pairing that had been destined. And it made her heart swell with pride and joy.

Louise was introduced to Marcus's parents as they approached the front pew of the modest-looking church. Mrs. Jefferson was being embraced warmly by everyone in the congregation in a celebration of her hopeful prognosis. More than one parishioner wondered aloud if it was possible that her good news and the arrival of their new, magnetic pastor was more than a mere coincidence. The congregation adored him, and they believed him capable of anything. Even a miracle.

They shed visible tears of rapture as the pastor made his way up to the pulpit and gazed down upon his reverential flock. Louise looked at the man's face for the first time. She, too, immediately believed that this man was capable of anything. Her mahogany skin flushed ghostly white, and she felt a sharp chill go up her spine. Her trembling hands desperately reached for Arima's. She pulled her astonished and confused granddaughter to her feet and dragged her hastily to the front door. This was the last time that Marcus had been seen or heard from by them for the past two days. The pair disappeared through the white door and into the sultry evening air as the Pastor looked on knowingly.

The subtle approach isn't going to work, the Pastor thought to himself as he launched into his animated and uplifting sermon.

Marcus had not heard another person's voice for two days. Following the Sunday evening service, Marcus said goodbye to his parents and immediately began walking towards Arima's house in order to find out what may have been wrong with her grandmother. He turned a corner and was greeted by a white man who asked him for a light. He felt a sharp pain on the top of his head.

He woke up to the sensation of drowning and lay there gasping for his life. For the past two days, there had been no talking. There had been only constant waterboarding and beatings. He would be dragged from his chair, laid at an angle on a flat board, and have water poured over his face. This was done continuously until Marcus was praying for death. He would be taken back to his chair, strapped down, and beaten with clubs throughout his face and body. He could feel, then hear his bones crack with each subsequent blow. His fingers had been snapped, meticulously. His ankles had been broken. His ribs had been broken. His jaw had been broken. His nose had been broken. His spirit had been broken.

He sat there, bound to his chair, weeping, when he finally heard another person's voice. The voice caused him to feel both confusion and bone-chilling fear simultaneously. It was the slithery voice of the Pastor.

"Hello, Marcus," the Pastor began with a calm arrogance. "I'm so sorry about all of this, but it is quite necessary, as you shall soon see. I'm going to remove your hood now and you and I are going to come to an...agreement."

The Pastor removed the hood from Marcus's battered face and his swollen eyes stared in disbelief at the blurred, smug expression of the Pastor.

"Let me explain what is happening, Marcus," the Pastor began again. "From the moment that I was born, I knew that I was destined for great things. That I was *destined* to serve a great power. Following the, well, we'll say, tragic death of my parents, I was taken in by a group. This group worships the great Vetis, the Tempter of the Holy. They showed me the mark of Vetis on the top of my head and told me that I was destined to be a revered general in Vetis's army. That Vetis would one day come to Earth and hold dominion over all of his Earth-bound subjects. And that Vetis would also wage a glorious war against the afterlife, against Enlightenment, and hold dominion over that as well. That Vetis was destined to dominate *this* life *and* the afterlife. And that *I* was one of his most important disciples who was *destined* to rule by his side.

"I was told that I would have two most important tasks. One task was to convert those on this earth who believed themselves to be *holy* to become *unholy*. To take their *pure devotion* to their chosen deity and *twist it* into a blind devotion to hatred and violence towards others. I am one of many who have this task and this battle has been waging for centuries. We have been so close to victory in the past twenty years, only to be beaten back again and again. We do not yet have enough numbers. We have yet to convert enough *souls* from light to dark. We do not yet have enough *power* to topple the world's democracies and replace them with brutal dictators that are humbled servants of Vetis. But this battle wages on and the dream is still quite alive.

"Which brings me to my second most important task. I was to sire a daughter. A most powerful daughter who would fight alongside me. And our unholy union would tip the scales of power in favor of *us*, the disciples of Vetis. I have two daughters. The first was born in Wisconsin and she has been…a disappointment. In fact, she has become quite a formidable adversary against us. But her mother will take care of her…in due time.

"My second daughter just came of age and has recently become aware of her great powers. She has the ability to absorb dark souls who are trapped here and enable them to use her body to commit the most glorious crimes against humanity. Or she can destroy them. Of course, the second daughter that I speak of is Arima."

Marcus began weeping uncontrollably as he prayed for this nightmare to end. But his prayers were not answered, and he was forced to continue to listen to the Pastor's deplorable diatribe.

"I must bring Arima into our fold. I had wanted her mother as well, but her soul was too pure to corrupt, so I sacrificed her to Vetis. I split her open so that her blood would be absorbed by the altar of Vetis and then I beheaded her and placed her head on a spike. Not unlike what I did to your previous pastor of your church. I needed a way to get to you so that I could use you to get to Arima. Plus, it gives me the opportunity to corrupt an entirely different group of believers. They are all so easily influenced. They all want to believe so badly that they are deserving of a grand afterlife. Some are. Most aren't. Most are greedy and self-serving bastards who would sell their own daughter out just for a small taste of the good life. Most are exactly like me. So I murdered your former pastor. And that is what will happen to Arima as well if she does not join me by my side. And that is where you come in.

"I am indeed sorry for having put you through such an…inconvenience, but, you see, you needed to understand what we…what *I* am capable of. You *must* understand that what I am telling you is true. You *must* understand that if you fail me, then the fate of Arima's mother will also be yours. And that fate will be Arima's as well.

"So how can you be of assistance to me you may want to ask? She has fallen in love with you. You hold great influence over her. You will call her and your family and tell them that you are fine. Tell them that you have gone on a trip and that you won't be back for some time. During that time, I will nurture you. I will *nurture* and *heal* both your body and your soul. You will join me and you will work with me on bringing Arima to me. You will deliver her to where she belongs. Once both your body and soul are…

healed…shall we say…you will *murder* Arima's grandmother. She must be eliminated in order to have any chance of success. I would like to do that old bitch in myself, but it is better this way. You are able to get close to her. I am not, as you may have noticed at Sunday evening's service.

"Then you will seduce Arima and bring her to me. Arima will be quite weakened by the loss of her dear, old grandmother and she will be easily influenced. You will bring her to me and then…well…*I* will do what *I* do best. I will turn her light into darkness. And then, together, we will re-engage in the war that is being fought. And with Arima's help, we shall be victorious in turning this damnable democracy into a mindless herd of followers of Vetis's chosen pawn of a dictator. And once this country falls, the other democracies throughout the world will easily fall as well. And then Vetis shall arrive, and we shall collect all of our fallen dark souls and destroy Enlightenment itself!

"So, Marcus…what do you say? Are you going to help me or…should I just slit your throat right now and do this on my own?"

Every cell in every part of Marcus's being was throbbing with pain. Physical pain. Mental pain. Emotional pain. Spiritual pain. He wanted to resist. He wanted to spit in the Pastor's eye. He wanted to break free from his chains and beat this arrogant, selfish, sadistic bully with his hands until he was nothing more than bloody pulp. But he knew that he could not do any of that at this moment. He could willingly sacrifice himself. What he could *not* allow was Arima to be sacrificed as well. He had to buy some time and reach deeply into his personal faith and pray that he would not be converted like the mindless others. He must accept this now and pray for strength and the opportunity to fight another day. He was disgusted with himself as he heard his beleaguered voice come out of his split and bloody lips. "Y-yes. I will help you."

———

"And that, my child, is your father," Louise stated solemnly through her tears to her astonished granddaughter. "That is your father and that is what he is capable of. I have prayed that we would never see his hideous face ever again. But he is here. He is here for *you*. You cannot help Marcus now. If that vile man has him, then he's already gone, one way or another. We must get you far away, my dearest. We must hide you from him. He will try to get you to join him. And, if you do, it may mean the end of humanity as we know it. And if you don't, he will destroy you. I have already lost my beloved daughter and I will be damned if I lose you, too. Please, Arima. Let us go to the bus station and get you far away from here. And *not* New York! Perhaps the West Coast. I know some people there that can protect you. Please, my child. Pack a bag and let us go now."

Arima wiped tears from her eyes. The fear that her grandmother's story had instilled in her was turning into burning rage. And that burning rage was joined by a steely resolve.

"No," Arima bluntly stated with a blazing determination. "No. I *will* find Marcus. I *will not* have that fine man that I love be sacrificed. I *will not* allow him to be harmed because of me. I must find him, and I must destroy my father. All I need is to know how. I just need to figure out a plan. I just need…"

Arima's sentence was interrupted by an evil voice coming from a darkened, protruding, demonic face that was oozing from out of the scenic harbor painting. *Heh, heh, heh…perhaps I could be of some assistance? For a price, of course. Heh, heh, heh.*

Chapter 13

Wrong on Multiple Levels

Howard had not felt so alive in centuries. It had been 245 years, to be exact, since he was able to feel movement of his legs. He relished the warm breeze that he could feel whisking through Arima's braids and gazed in wonder through her mahogany eyes at the sites that was 2034 New Orleans. The neon signs. The bustling people. The electric lights. The motorcars. He was in complete ecstasy and didn't believe he could ever be happier. He immediately realized he was wrong about that as he saw a local shop as Arima's body strolled by with purpose down the busy street.

Here. Stop here. It looks perfect, Howard stated lasciviously to Arima's soul. *Yes, this place is amazing* he said gleefully as they entered the building. He excitedly gazed around the store as though he were a child making his first visit to a candy store. Everywhere he looked there was black leather. He literally squealed with delight as he perused the cornucopia of whips, shackles, hoods, paddles, and other...accessories. *What is this?* Howard squealed out again as he gazed upon a large strap-on phallus.

Oh, my God, that is so pervy! Howard, calm the hell down, Arima silently said to him. *I can feel you getting...aroused...and it's really creepy. Although, I have to admit, there is some fun stuff in here.*

I can't help it, Howard immediately replied as he was barely able to control his excitement. *This shop is...my dream. Oh, how much fun I could have had in my day with my little slave playthings if I had all of this. Oh, my. All of the blood. The screaming. The tears. The cu...*

Howard! Arima screamed at him.

I mean, heh, heh, heh, Howard hastily responded in an attempt to back track from his sadistic fantasies. *Not that I would ever do anything like that again. No, I have learned over these centuries. I have learned that slavery is wrong. I have learned that beating innocent people and raping innocent women is wrong. I have learned that I must change my ways in order to get into Enlightenment and be released from that damned painting. I'm sorry, Arima. Please forgive me.*

Bullshit, Arima replied sternly. *I cannot only hear you, but I can feel your intentions and you're the same sadistic prick that you've always been and the only reason why I've allowed you into my soul is so you can help me get my boyfriend back. I love him so much and that is the only thing that could ever allow me to let someone as sleazy as you into me. We have a deal. I will let you help me, and the powers of Enlightenment will decide if you have redeemed yourself or not. In exchange, I have promised that I won't burn the painting with your soul in it. But if you try to completely overtake me or do anything out of line, I will banish you once again into that painting and fry your racist, sexist ass! Got it? Now pick out what you need for this and let's get Marcus back!*

Yeah, yeah, yeah, I got it, Howard replied in a defeated tone. *You are so much more powerful than your ancestors, that I would never dream of trying to completely control you. You will allow me to control your body so that I can have fun with your father, the Pastor. But you must be awake for this, Arima. You will see everything that I do. Do you understand? Oh, this looks fun,* Howard concluded as Arima's hand grasped the handle of a paddle with metal studs protruding from it.

Don't worry. I may not want to do this shit myself, but I'm starting to enjoy being a voyeur. You do what you want. I'll let you know if you're going too far. But in this case, I don't think that's possible. I think we need one of these, too, Arima finished as she picked up a multi-tasseled motorcycle whip.

Now you're getting the idea, heh, heh, heh, Howard sneered as he looked at the sizes of the black zippered hoods.

The hot soup stung Marcus's split lips as he eagerly took it in and swallowed. He had not eaten in three days, and he welcomed the sustenance despite from whom it came.

"There now, Marcus," the Pastor's voice stated with a sinister arrogance. "That's good. Very good. The healing has begun. First, your body will be nourished and healed. Then your soul will be nourished and healed. Soon you will see that what we are doing is right. It is just. Now, one of *your* kind certainly will never be able to sit alongside our glorious Vetis. But you will be rewarded for being such a loyal subject. You will be rewarded for bringing Arima to me. You will be allowed to live a comfortable life with your parents. And that, my dear friend, is as good as it could ever be for your kind. The rest of your people and many others will die…viciously. But you, my friend, will live to tell the tale. Here, how about another bite?"

Marcus swallowed hard. Partially to quell his starvation and partially to ward off the tears that were once again welling in his beaten eyes. He was still too broken physically and mentally to put up any sort of resistance. And he knew that he would be in that condition for some time. He said a silent prayer as another scalding bite of broth slid down his welcoming throat. He prayed for the strength to resist this vile man's indoctrination. He prayed that he would be able to join the fight against this deplorable movement. But mostly he prayed that Arima would remain safely out of her father's twisted grasp.

His prayers were suddenly vanquished as he heard his love's voice from behind the bed that he was lying in.

"Hey, there…um…Dad," Arima's smooth, casual voice was heard. But instead of being comforted by it, Marcus was filled with feelings of dread and remorse. She was alone and he was completely unable to assist her. Why had she come here? Why had she offered herself up as a sacrificial lamb? His heart sank even lower as he heard Arima's explanation.

"So, Dad…I know what you're up to. Grams told me everything. She told me about how you are a follower of Vetis and how you all plan on conquering the world's democracies by converting holy souls into unholy souls. She told me that once that is done, the unholy souls will then engage in a battle with Enlightenment. And she told me that once Enlightenment is conquered, Vetis will rule the world and the afterlife.

"I understand what is happening. I see it on the news. I now know that the international autocratic movement that has been trying to topple the world's democracies, including ours, is not being done in the name of God. It is being done in the name of Vetis. The people who believe themselves to be holy and patriotic have instead been duped into becoming the pawns of a power-hungry demon.

"I also understand that I am destined to engage in this battle alongside my father. I don't know that I agree with all of this, but I know that I'm simply not powerful enough to fight against you and your forces in this war. Not after what I see you've done to Marcus. So, what I'm saying is that I'm in. But on one condition. You leave Marcus and Grams and my friends alone. Just let them be. If you promise to do that, then I will do what you need me to do. Do we have a deal?"

"Why…yes," a pleasantly surprised Pastor responded as he looked upon his black leather-clad daughter. "Yes, my dear child, we have a deal. My, if I had known it would be that easy, I wouldn't have…well…we won't discuss that now. You can sit at my side, and we can tend to your Marcus together. You can even keep him if you wish. You and I shall heal him and then we shall re-engage in this war. Oh, Arima, you have made me so happy. Together, we will be quite powerful. Together, we will be able to tip the scales in favor of Vetis. Together, we will be able to take out the various freedom-fighting forces throughout the world. Oh, my dearest child, this may be the happiest day of my life."

"Yeah, for me, too," Arima replied affectionately. "I've always had this strange feeling that I was meant to be with my father. I am not my mother nor am I my grandmother. I realize that now. I was meant for bigger things. I was meant to be in the warm embrace of my father. I was meant to be a warrior."

"Yes, you were, my child," the Pastor stated confidently as he strode toward Arima and wrapped his arms around her figure in a seemingly pre-ordained embrace.

Arima's eyes glanced over at her immobilized and tearful Marcus. She gave him a slight smile and wink before taking a dagger from behind her waist. She lifted the dagger, then plunged it into the back of her father.

The Pastor screamed in agony and began flailing around as he attempted to pull the dagger from his upper back. "You little bitch!" he screamed at Arima who was taking items out of her black duffle bag. "I will rip you apart for this!"

"No, you won't," came a sinister voice from Arima's mouth. "Heh, heh,

heh. Arima is not in control at the moment. Oh. she is here. She is watching quite intently. And she can stop me at any moment, can't you, dear"?

Yup, Arima's soul replied to that of Howard's. *But I won't. He disgusts me. Damn, Howard. I have to admit. You're pretty good at this. I never would have thought of all that stuff to say to him. I wouldn't be able to keep it together long enough. I wouldn't have been able to kiss his ass like that. I just don't have it in me to be so deceitful.*

"Which is why you have me, my dear," Howard said aloud through Arima's voice as he cracked a bullwhip around the Pastor's ankles and pulled, causing the Pastor to fall backwards. The Pastor shrieked in pain once again as the knife plunged further into his back.

"Oh, that felt good," Howard sneered as he paced around the Pastor's struggling body. "I see I haven't lost my touch with the whip. Or have I? Perhaps just a bit more practice. Just to be sure."

Arima's body began lashing at the Pastor's face with the whip. Deep lacerations immediately began oozing blood as the harsh leather sliced his face repeatedly. Arima's voice cackled with a sinister glee as she turned the Pastor over, dropped his pants and began beating his behind repeatedly with the metal studs of the paddle. Bloody pock marks covered his posterior as he was struck repeatedly. Specks of blood covered the paddle and Arima's joyfully sadistic face. Then, the beating suddenly stopped.

Arima's body went back to her black duffle bag. As Howard's attention was preoccupied with finding his greatest treasure, the Pastor reached up to a nearby table and pulled the tablecloth until a lit kerosene lamp fell next to him. Howard pulled the strap-on phallus from the duffle and exclaimed in delight, "Ah, here it is! Oh, what fun we shall now have, won't we, Pastor? Or shall I call you...Peggy? Heh, heh, heh".

The panicked Pastor looked at Arima's possessed body, triumphantly holding the strap-on above her head, then flung the kerosene lamp onto the immobile body of Marcus.

Marcus's shirt immediately caught fire and Arima screamed, "No!" Having retaken control over her body, she flew towards the howling Marcus. She grabbed a blanket and began beating the flames until they were extinguished. Arima looked down upon the slightly burned chest of her love. She looked at his broken body. She looked at his tattered face. And she wept.

Dammit Arima! Howard's voice yelled to her soul. *He is gone! I was not done with him yet! You have let him escape!*

"I-I-I don't care," Arima tearfully replied. "I have my Marcus back. I'll deal with that old bastard later." A confused Marcus smiled up at his love and began weeping. Arima gently ran her hands over his tortured body so as not to cause him any more pain. She got down on her knees, laid her head tenderly upon his chest and wept along with him.

"C'mon," she said to Marcus after she had regained her composure. "Let's get you out of here and get you some cheeseburgers. And some fries. And some onion rings. And maybe a milkshake."

Marcus did not mind the stabbing pain in his ribs as he laughed for the first time in days.

Louise Azar arrived at the abandoned church with several of her colleagues. "Very nicely done, ladies," she said to the group. "Thank you for helping my granddaughter track down these souls. It is a shame that that bastard got away, but now we know what we are dealing with. And we know that we can wound him. We know that *you* can wound him, Arima. And if you can *wound* him, then you can *kill* him. And you shall, one day. All right, ladies, let's get this poor boy home. He has a long recovery ahead of him."

As Arima and the soul of Howard were leaving the old church, Howard said in a jealous tone, *What is all this about you* can hurt him *and you* can kill him? *I'm the one that did all of the work! You were just along for the ride!*

"Howard, have you noticed that despite your helping me that you have not been called to Enlightenment"? Arima said to Howard aloud so that all could hear. "Do you know why that is, Howard? It is because you don't get into Enlightenment solely because of your deeds. It is the intent *behind* the deeds that gets you in. It is the *purity* of the intention. You can *kill* someone and still get in if your intentions were good. If you committed murder because you were selflessly protecting someone else, for example. The murder isn't the point. It is the reason *behind* the murder that is the point. And you could donate ten million dollars to build a wing on a children's hospital and *not* get in. Why? Because if your intent for that donation was for your own personal fame or increased power or more money for yourself later, then the gesture doesn't count. It wasn't done out of *selflessness*. It was done out of *selfishness*. So, it isn't your *actions* that get you to Enlightenment. It is the intent *behind* your actions. You would do well to think about that if...and I *do* mean if...you ever get this chance again."

Louise burst out laughing as she heard her granddaughter conclude her lecture with, "Oh, and one more thing. I don't care *who* is in control. I am *not* going to screw my own father...or anyone *else* for that matter...up the ass. I will *not* have my body used for that. That's just wrong on soooo many levels. Man, I can't wait to get home and get baked. I wonder if Jess has made any more cookies."

Chapter 14

The Fury of Redemption...or is That Furry?

For the next two months, Arima had very little time to enjoy her favorite pastime, which resulted in each week's groceries lasting considerably longer. When she wasn't busy helping Marcus's Pops care for his son and his ever-strengthening wife, she was studying with her grandmother in honing her abilities. She was learning how to focus. She was learning how to control her emotions and impulses. She was learning how to trust her instincts. And she was learning what a great responsibility it was that she had inherited.

And then there were her responsibilities at the morgue. She was asked, along with other employees, to pull a few extra shifts by Clyde while Marcus was recovering, which Arima enthusiastically agreed to. She was working sixty to seventy hours per week and giving the extra income to Marcus so that he could continue to fulfill his financial responsibilities to his parents' household.

And, of course, there were the trapped souls. At least one recently departed soul would ask Arima for her assistance to move on to Enlightenment each week. The Ropers selflessly assisted Arima by becoming her assistants. They knew that with each soul that Arima helped, their turn to redeem themselves and be allowed into Enlightenment was being delayed. But the Ropers had grown to love Arima as if she were their own and they were resolute in helping her for as long as she needed and in whatever way that they could. They would screen the applicants vying for Arima's special abilities, prioritize them, then make their suggestions to Arima as to how she might be able to help them.

Mr. Roper would greet the newly trapped soul and say, *Thank you for coming in. You may refer to me as Mr. Roper and this is my beautiful wife, Mrs. Roper. We shall be conducting your interview today on behalf of Arima.* Then he would begin the standardized questions that had been developed by his wife, who would be taking copious mental notes during the interview.

What is your name?

How did you die?

Why are you being kept here?

What is it that you feel you need to do to redeem yourself in order to move on to Enlightenment?

If nothing, who is it that you are here to watch over or protect?

If no one, what evil deed do you believe you need to exact retribution for and to whom? What means would you like to use to exact this retribution?

If you were stranded on a desert island, what five albums would you take with you? (An answer including Kid Rock was an immediate disqualifier. An answer including Bruce Springsteen, REM, David Bowie, Southern Culture on the Skids or The Cramps shot the applicant to the top of the list.)

If Arima chooses you to inhabit her body, do you swear that you will not use her body for anything untoward outside of the assigned mission? Untoward acts may include but are not limited to racist comments or actions, sexist comments or actions, homophobic or transphobic comments or actions, any form of brutality against an innocent, eating fruit, or having her put on a strap-on phallus and having anal intercourse with another person.

The interview would conclude with, *Very well. Thank you for coming in and for your interest in Arima's services. We will be in touch. And remember, all further communication is to be done through us. She is quite busy, and you must not contact Arima directly or you will not be considered.*

The anxious spirit would then take its place somewhere in the limbo that was the city morgue and wait.

The Ropers would consult with Arima who would then decide who to assist. Mrs. Roper would announce the spirit's name, who would then be allowed to have a personal consultation with Arima. She would sit in her beaten leather office chair, twiddling her thumbs, as she listened intently to the spirit's emphatic pleas for assistance. She looked like a godfather who was holding court and would frequently conclude with, "But you must understand that there may come a time that I ask a favor of *you*, even if you have been allowed into Enlightenment. Do you agree?"

The appreciative spirit would always joyfully agree and Arima would begin her work. Most of the cases were rather easy to resolve.

There was the bank executive who had gotten himself into financial difficulties and framed a co-worker for his embezzlement. He inhabited Arima's body and through her hands typed out and sent a letter to the District Attorney that detailed all of the evidence that would clear the wrongfully accused and implicate himself. His smiling spirit wept as he elevated out of Arima's body and ascended to Enlightenment.

There was the man who was murdered by his wife out of self-defense as he once again lunged at her with the intention of beating her. Immediately upon feeling his soul lift from his body, he felt his wife's pain and anguish. He also felt genuine remorse for his dastardly actions against the woman that he professed to love. Based on his authentic contrition, Arima took on his case and assisted him in locating the evidence of his crimes that he had hidden from his wife. This evidence included hospital records, phone records, recordings of their arguments, and pictures of her battered body. The evidence was placed into an envelope and sent to the prosecuting attorney. All charges against his wife were dropped, and she was able to collect his life insurance. He was admitted into Enlightenment but was sentenced to feel the pain and fear that his wife had experienced for all of eternity.

There was the young man who was tragically stricken down by cancer. His husband was despondent over the loss and vowed to never love again. The spirit loved his husband so much that he knew that he could not ascend until he saw his husband smile and feel genuine joy again. He inhabited Arima's body and followed his husband around in order to see if he could locate someone that would make his grieving husband happy. Someone that he could love. He noticed a handsome barista and could feel his genuine concern and caring for his husband, so he had Arima purchase two tickets to a concert that he knew his husband would attend. One ticket was sent to his husband, with a letter of congratulations on winning the prize. The other ticket and letter were sent to the barista. The seats were located next to each other. As the spirit watched his husband through Arima's eyes leave the concert hall hand-in-hand with his new love, he blissfully wept, then ascended in peace.

Other cases were a bit more complicated and messier. There was a young woman who had become indoctrinated to hate other people that were not like her. She had been indoctrinated in these fanatically dangerous beliefs at a local church by a particular Pastor. She was assigned to a local regiment of neo-fascist Brownshirts. On the evening of her initiation, she watched in horror as three sadistic Brownshirts beat, raped, and murdered a twelve-year-old African-American girl. The revolting images shook her to her core, and she suddenly realized that what she was involved with was not the work of God. She believed it to be the work of Satan himself. She fled the scene as the girl's battered body was being hung from a flashing stop sign.

She immediately went to a bus station and was standing in line to purchase a ticket to anywhere but there when a man in a brown shirt came up from behind and thrust something hard and round into her back. "Just take it easy. We just need to talk," the man stated quietly as he led her out of the bus station and into his waiting car. He drove her to an abandoned lot. And then, she was forced to endure what the little girl had endured. For hours. She finally succumbed as she bled out from the final laceration that was purposefully inflicted between her legs.

She was taken to the morgue, and she sat quietly and watched as the three Brownshirts that had murdered the little girl were destroyed by Arima. It was then that she decided that it was safe to reveal herself. It was then that she realized that she had to have justice for her murder. Brutal justice.

"Oh yeah. I'll *definitely* help you. My body is yours. You do to that bastard anything that you want," Arima stated with resolve to the spirit named Lillian.

Lillian watched through Arima's eyes as her murderer staggered out of a local tavern. She watched him sway for three blocks before turning up on a gravel driveway. His hip caught the back end of an old, rusted car and he fell over, laughing. He looked up and saw the furious face of Arima and said through his drunken chuckles, "Bitch, don't you know where you're at? You'd better get along now, lil' piggy, or else I'm-a-gonna beat you. Your kind don't belong here, so if'n you ain't down the street before I get up, then you're gonna end up in the river. Y'know…after I have some fun with ya first."

The Brownshirt's threat was moot. He never had the chance to get up. Arima could feel the intensity of Lillian's rage as she took a hammer from behind her back and struck the man in the temple with it. Her murderer could only scream as Lillian used Arima's body to straddle him and beat him in the face repeatedly with the hammer until it looked like children's play dough that had melted in the unforgiving heat of the sun.

Too much? Lillian's smiling soul asked Arima as she began to elevate upwards.

"Nope," Arima immediately replied as she wiped the man's blood from her face. "Maybe not *enough* for a prick like him. It was nice to meet you, Lillian. I hope we will meet again someday."

Arima was unable to help everyone, however. There was a sleazy local politician who had lied and cheated in order to cover up his affair with an adult film actress. Following the in-depth consultation, Arima determined that his crimes and narcissistic intentions behind those crimes were so far-reaching and entrenched that she could not help him, so she banished his spirit into a men's urinal. "Well, since I have seen that you're into golden showers, this should make you happy for all eternity," she said, laughing to the tantrum-throwing spirit as she placed him in the urinal. She returned to the morgue and said to the Ropers, "Hey, guys, you're doing a really great job but how 'bout tightening up the interview process a bit? That dick was a complete waste of my time."

And finally, there was the easiest case of them all. Or so it initially seemed. There was an elderly lady who passed away following a sudden stroke. She had lived her life selflessly and graciously. She had ushered three loving and admirable children into the world and overseen the growth of five beautiful grandchildren. Everyone adored her, even those that found it difficult to love anyone. This included her one-year-old cat, LucyFur. No one would take LucyFur in and the poor soul had been abandoned at the no-kill animal shelter. The old lady could not move on until she found a loving home for her beloved pet.

"Well, this one's easy enough. I guess I just adopted a cat!" Arima declared. The old lady's spirit smiled and thanked Arima as she elevated to Enlightenment.

"Wow, guys," Arima said aloud to the Ropers. "I feel really good about myself. I've really done some good things with my powers. And now, the universe has rewarded me with a sweet-ass cat! Who says there's no such thing as karma?"

Arima took LucyFur home and soon realized three things. She realized that there was no such thing as karma. She realized why no one was willing to adopt this animal because she also realized why this energetic and seemingly demonic furball had been named "LucyFur."

Upon returning home with her purring bundle of joy, she placed the grey and white long-haired cat down on the living room floor and said, "Okay, baby. I gotta go outside and bring your stuff in that I ordered, okay? So, just sit here and be sweet and don't get into anything."

As Arima was retrieving a litter box, bag of cat litter, cat food, and an overstuffed bag of cat toys from her front porch, her housemates arrived home. "Hey, sweetie, what's all this, then?" an intrigued Jamie inquired.

"Okay, don't freak out, you guys," Arima defensively answered. "I just adopted a cat. But she's super sweet and super cute and super mellow. She just sat on my lap and purred the entire bus ride home. I'll totally take care of her, and she won't be any trouble, okay?"

"Oh, fine," a slightly annoyed Jessie replied. "Just keep that thing away from me. Me and cats don't exactly jive, all right?"

"Yup, not a problem," Arima enthusiastically declared. "C'mon! I want to introduce you to her! I just know that you're gonna love her!"

Arima excitedly opened the front door. Four human jaws dropped simultaneously as they saw LucyFur sitting innocently in the middle of... absolute carnage.

The few curtains that had been allowed to remain hanging were torn to shreds. One entire couch cushion had been disemboweled. There were ripped newspapers and magazines covering the coffee table, floor, and furniture as though there had been an explosive ticker-tape parade. Two lamps and three vases were shattered on the floor. The roll of toilet paper was no longer recognizable as toilet paper. And there was a trail of tattered underwear coming from Cliff and Jessie's bedroom.

Jessie said nothing as she bent over and picked up a pair of her now crotchless panties. Cliff tried to lighten the moment by saying, "y'know, I kinda like them that way." Her daggered gaze made him quickly realize that it would be wise not to utter another sound and he obediently dropped his head to the floor. She stared silently at the cat, then at Arima in furious disbelief.

Jessie calmed herself slightly and asked curtly through her gritted teeth, "So, what's the cat's name?"

Arima meekly responded without daring to look up at her friend, "Um… LucyFur."

"No shit, huh? Can I freak out *now*?" Jessie tersely replied before making her way to her bedroom and slamming the door.

Chapter 15

Blood is an Acquired Taste

"Shut up! Just shut up!" the Pastor screamed at the dark purple smog that was billowing in the corner of a run-down evangelical church in West Texas. "I'm just now able to walk upright without much pain! I barely escaped Arima's attack on me! So I don't need you to tell me that I have failed! I don't need you to tell me how strong she is! I don't need you to tell me that she must be destroyed! I know all of that! What about you? Where the hell have *you* been? I see that our daughter is still successfully battling our forces. What are you going to do about *that?*"

Yes, Pastor, the nasally sinister voice began emanating from the copper headed purple cloud. *I am well aware of your failures. You really are quite good at getting yourself beaten, aren't you? And I am well aware of our daughter's exploits. Getting to her is much more complicated for me in this form. I either have to be welcomed in by someone such as Arima and be allowed to take over their body or I must find someone who hates our daughter as much as I do. If I can find such a dark soul, then I can enter them without their knowing. My hate will combine with theirs and they will be completely unaware that I have possessed them and that I can take control of them at any time.*

So what have I been doing? Searching, you fool. Searching for someone with that same intense hatred for our little whore daughter. I had thought that it would be quite easy. She has made so many enemies. Unfortunately, she has succeeded in eliminating most of those enemies. And she has this unique quality to build support and loyalty from those around her. That is her special ability. People grow to love her and will do anything for her, despite her rather crass demeanor. That is her gift...along with her unbridled tenacity. So, Pastor, I have been searching for a body and soul to inhabit.

And I have found one. In a mental institution in New York. A former friend of hers. Our daughter betrayed her by stealing her precious children away and recruiting them into her army. She despises our daughter. But not yet as much as I do. Despite the betrayal, she still harbors feelings for our daughter. So, I must beat her down. I must invade her dreams every night and methodically extinguish any feelings of love or respect that she has for our daughter. I must then allow her hatred to grow. And once I have done that, I will be able to possess her soul and take control of her body. But this will take time. Years perhaps. But once I have accomplished this, it will be as simple as pulling a trigger with my host's finger. And our little bitch daughter will be no more. And her soul will float out into limbo where I can destroy her once again, for all time.

But Arima must be taken out before then. If she will not join us, then she must be destroyed. Our daughter's spirit will never be vanquished as long as Arima is here in human form. Arima can serve as our daughter's gateway back here. Back to the battle. Back to us. And they will be together. These half-sisters must never be allowed to join forces. With Arima's abilities and our daughter's loyal army and tenacity, all will be lost. So, Pastor, take your little bitch out!

"Oh, I plan to," the Pastor replied through a dark chuckle as he looked down at his disfigured hands while still feeling a sharp pain from the healing knife wound in his back. "Oh, I am *definitely* taking out that little bitch. But I'm going to make her *suffer* first. I'm going to beat her down emotionally before I kill her. I am going to cause her so much mental anguish that she will be too weak to fight me and will welcome her own death. I am going to violently murder every person that she loves. One by one. I'll start with her best friends. Then her lover. And finally, I will find a way to take out that bitch grandmother of hers. Then maybe I can leave this damned church. Maybe *then* I will be able to go outside and feel the sun on my face again. But not until her grandmother is gone.

"I had no idea that her grandmother and those other bitches in their little voodoo cult could track souls. That they could track *my* soul. And I know that they are searching for me. They are like a pack of psychic bloodhounds. I have had to be very careful so that they cannot find me. I have had to insulate myself in this damnable church and surround myself with the symbols of Vetis in order to conceal my whereabouts. But once I am outside, and away from the symbols' protection, I will be vulnerable, and they will be able to find me. So, as much as I would like to do these little bastards in myself, I will have to depend on my minions to do my bidding for me."

The Pastor motioned to one of his Brownshirts and said to the skin-headed, hate tattoo covered dullard, "Go after the little blonde first. Do whatever you want to her. Have as much fun as you like. Just make it... *messy*, heh, heh, heh."

———

"Dammit Arima!" an increasingly frustrated Jessie yelled out. "Would you *please* do something about this damned cat? Now it's eaten my slippers!"

"Sorry, Jess," Arima replied with an embarrassed tone. "C'mon, LucyFur. Let's go upstairs and get you a snack. *Please* leave Jess's stuff alone, okay?"

Cliff, Jamie, and Marcus were sitting on the couch, attempting not to burst out laughing as Jessie came into the living room and yelled, "Why does that cat *hate* me so much? What the hell did I ever do to *her*? Why does she only destroy *my* stuff? Oh, forget it! I've gotta go to work! But I'm adding all this stuff up Arima! You're going to pay me back for everything that little menace has destroyed! Got it?"

"Yeah," Arima's beleaguered voice came from upstairs. "I'm sorry, Jess, I'll keep working with her."

Jessie and LucyFur did not have a love/hate relationship. Jessie and LucyFur had a hate/hate relationship. The pair would literally hiss at one another whenever their paths crossed. For some reason only known to her, LucyFur had decided to take her anger and unbridled energy out only on Jessie's person and belongings. Children's locks had to be placed on all of the kitchen cabinet doors to prevent LucyFur from getting in them and destroying Jessie's boxes of tea, crackers, or cereal. She would watch attentively as groceries were put away and would eat only Jessie's food when given the opportunity. She had figured out how to jump up and turn the doorknob on Jessie and Cliff's bedroom door. Jessie would arrive home to find her tops, jeans, and delicates strewn about the room in tatters. Cliff's items were never bothered. When Jessie arrived home, she would have to cautiously open the front door. She would reach her hand inside and turn on the living room light. With trepidation, she would dart her eyes around the room to see where the inevitable attack would come from. Seeing no imminent danger, she would exhale in relief, enter the living room, and take a few steps. From out of nowhere, Jessie would then feel LucyFur's sharp claws on her ankles, calves, or shoulder. Jessie was in a state of constant anxiety. LucyFur was in a state of constant bemusement, and she would sit on another housemate's lap, contently purring while staring Jessie down as if she were taunting her.

LucyFur may have been vicious to Jessie, but she was extremely protective of anyone else in the house. She would watch over Arima, in particular. She would give Arima a mew of warning if she were about to step on something that could make her trip. She would claw Marcus's back if she confused Arima's moans of pleasure for pleas for help. And she would intensely eye anyone who came to the door. If LucyFur sensed that the interloper was a threat in any way, she would leap up and attack their face. Within one month of LucyFur's residing there, the household was no longer able to get a pizza delivered.

Jessie arrived home from work. Realizing that no one else would be there except for the demonic cat, she once again cautiously unlocked and opened the front door. Her anxiety increased as she scanned the room for the furball of fury. She checked her pantlegs to ensure that they were completely over her heavy combat boots. She zipped up her heavy coat, put the hood over her head and sprinted toward her bedroom. She shrieked as LucyFur lunged at her from on top of the door frame. She made it into her bedroom and slammed the door.

As she was sitting on her bed, shaking, she heard the doorbell ring. Her heart was pounding as she wondered how she would be able to navigate the cat's ninja-esque attacks in order to answer the door. She then heard the person pounding on the door and Jessie decided that it just wasn't worth it. She wasn't expecting anyone, so it just wasn't her problem. She curled up on her bed and shut her eyes. Then, whoever was at the door *became* her problem.

She heard the front door open, then close. She heard heavy footsteps steadily approaching her room. She then saw an axe shatter her bedroom door. Jessie screamed and rolled off of her bed as splinters of wood exploded around her. A man with a shaved head, brown shirt, and Nazi tattoos was laughing as he picked Jessie up by her golden hair and threw her onto the bed. He took out a knife and slashed through her heavy coat.

Jessie instinctively kicked the man in his balls, rolled off of the bed and ran toward the front door. The man caught up to her, grabbed her once again by her hair and threw her across the room into a glass cabinet. A dazed Jessie looked up at the man with shards of glass protruding from her pleading and bloody face.

"Oh, I'm gonna have *fun* with you," the sadistic man said in a devilish voice as he lasciviously licked the blade of his knife. Jessie put her hands in front of her wounded face and clenched her eyes shut as the man lumbered toward her. Jessie then heard a deep, persistent growl coming from the top of the shattered cabinet. She heard a man screaming and looked up.

LucyFur had straddled the man's face. She was shrieking in an unholy high pitch as she slashed at the man with her machete-like claws. The man was wailing as he futilely attempted to pull the frenzied animal from off of him.

He was finally able to grab the cat by its back fur and throw it across the room. LucyFur bounced off of the floor and in one leap was back on the man's face. She bit into his right eye. Blood and pus began shooting out of the man's socket as LucyFur pulled his eye out and swallowed it in one bite. She then sliced the man's left ear nearly off with one graceful swipe of her right paw.

The tortured man fell to the floor and began rolling around as the furious feline continued its frantic onslaught. Streams of blood were spattering around the room, creating thin red streaks on the furniture, decorations and walls. The room looked like a scene from a massacre. LucyFur finally bit deeply into the man's jugular. He could only lay there and helplessly gurgle as the cat continued in its vampiric quest and feasted on the man's fresh blood.

"Aw, man, that supper was great, Grams," Arima said as she, Cliff, Jamie, and Louise made their way up the front steps of the home. "Thanks so much for taking us out. That was the best steak I've ever had. Too bad we couldn't get ahold of Jess. I don't know why she didn't answer the phone. We just got the landline put in last week. Now all we have to do is track down a modem and she'll be back online. She'll have a lot fewer followers, but at least she'll be back online. Then all I have to do is get her and LucyFur to get along and everything will be back to normal. Maybe they could patch things up by sharing this medium rare steak that we brought home for her."

Cliff was the first to enter the house. He turned on the light as the other three made their way in. "Jess, you home?" Cliff yelled out before his eyes adjusted to the light. Everyone's jaws dropped as they surveyed the destruction. The cabinet was in shambles and there was glass everywhere. Newly bought lamps and vases were shattered on the floor. There were streaks of drying blood on every surface of the room, including the ceiling. The foursome walked around the couch and found a dead man with his throat ripped out. He was missing an eye and his face looked as though it had been through a shredding machine.

They then looked at the couch. Sitting silently and staring straight ahead with a shocked look on her face was Jessie. She still had shards of glass in her pretty face and was spattered with blood. LucyFur was sitting on her lap, purring and cleaning the blood from her saturated bushy tail with long strokes of her bright pink tongue.

"Jess...wh-what happened...are you all right?" a deeply concerned Arima asked.

LucyFur stopped cleaning and looked up at Arima. Jessie then looked up at Arima with bewildered eyes and simply said, "Okay. We can keep the cat."

Chapter 16

Seriously, How Many Family Secrets Do We Need?

Jamie, Cliff, and a rattled Jessie sat staring in amazement as they listened to Louise Azar explain why this violent attack had occurred. They listened about the demon, Vetis and how he was trying to conquer both the Earth and Enlightenment by converting the holy to do his sadistic bidding. They listened about how this was occurring in the United States through self-appointed fascist militias that were attempting to create a race war and systemically dominate local areas. They listened about how freedom fighters throughout the world were battling these anti-Christ, anti-patriots and, despite many recent victories, how this war was far from over. They listened about how the leaders of this demonic dictatorial movement were hand chosen servants of Vetis. They listened as Louise told them that Arima's father was one of them and that it was he who had sent Jessie's assailant.

Their eyes grew wider as Louise explained to them about Arima's abilities. Their jaws dropped further as they learned how Arima could not only communicate with souls who were trapped here but could allow them into her own soul and allow them to use her body to complete their earthly work so that they could move on to Enlightenment. They immediately started looking around the room in a panic as Louise concluded with, "And of course, this bastard's soul is still here, isn't it dear?"

"Yeah, that prick's still hanging around," Arima replied nonchalantly as she took the joint that she had been sharing from Marcus. "I'm too tired to mess with him right now, Grams. I just need to relax, have a snack, and get some rest. He isn't going anywhere, and he can't do any real harm except annoy the shit out of me. I'll destroy him in the morning."

At that moment, LucyFur sprang from Jessie's lap and lunged at the new curtain that was hanging in the living room front window. She shredded the curtain in a frenzy while growling deeply. She then bounced on top of the entertainment center and began wildly clawing at the air.

"Aw, dammit," Arima stated with resignation while exhaling a long plume of smoke. "LucyFur's picked up on that prick. If I don't do something tonight, she'll destroy the house...again." Arima got up from her chair, walked into the middle of the room, spread her arms, and said to her friends who were sitting behind her on the couch, "Okay, guys. Don't freak out. This shit's gonna get kinda freaky."

Arima's body began levitating off of the floor as she focused on connecting with the evil spirit and began drawing him in. She was the only one besides Louise who could hear him screaming. *Oh no, bitch! You're not going to suck me in! I'm going to stay here for eternity and haunt your Black ass! I'm going to taunt that cat and have her destroy this house over and over! And if you move, I'll do worse to whoever moves in here! You have no power over me! And I will find other souls like mine, and we will team up and we will destroy you! We will...*

Jamie, Cliff, and Jessie looked on with confused expressions as they heard Arima begin to chuckle and say to apparently no one, "That's the funny thing about you dark souls. You are all so overconfident. You have had so much success bullying others that you have never learned how to size up your opponents. You think that you can threaten and intimidate and rape and murder your way through any battle. You think that you're all-powerful. Even *after* you've just been taken out by a *cat*. But you *aren't* all-powerful. In fact, I can sense that you have no *real* power at all except a few haunting parlor tricks. *I* am the one that has the power over *you!* I do not need your permission to draw you in! I can suck you into my essence as easily as I can suck in another puff of smoke. And that's what I'm going to do. So be a good little fascist prick and come to Momma, heh, heh, heh."

The evil spirit was screaming as it was drawn into Arima's essence. It continued screaming until Arima conjured a metal clasp around its mouth and bound it by her envisioned metal shackles. Arima's body was convulsing violently in mid-air as she bound him within her essence. Her convulsing suddenly stopped, and her bare toes gently returned to the floor.

"Damn, baby," Marcus stated as he watched his love through his blood-shot eyes. "I don't know if I'm *ever* gonna get used to you doing that shit. But it's kinda cool that I have a girlfriend that has powers and shit."

"So, you aren't intimidated by me? It doesn't bother you that I'm the most powerful one in this relationship?" Arima stated playfully as she straddled Marcus's lap and smiled.

"Hell, no," Marcus replied through his chuckles. "What the hell do *I* care? You take care of these demons or whatever and I'll take care of the snacks. It's a match made in heaven…or Enlightenment…or whatever. Hey baby, this one's spent. You want me to roll another one?"

Arima beamed at her love and gave him a long kiss.

"What the hell is going on?" she heard Jamie ask quietly behind her.

Arima got off of Marcus's lap and said to her friends, "What is going on is that I now have this bastard trapped inside me. But he's like squirming around and shit and I can't relax, so I need to trap him somewhere else. Now, where to put you?"

Arima scanned the room looking for a suitable inanimate object to trap him in, then destroy. Finding nothing, her search led her to the coffee table. She smiled, relinquished the dark soul and banished him into a…rolling paper. "Yeah, baby," Arima stated light-heartedly to Marcus. "Let's roll another one. And use *that* paper. We're gonna all *smoke* this bastard."

Arima and Louise chuckled to one another as they passed the joint around the room while listening to the tormented screams of the trapped spirit who was being painfully destroyed with each successive drag. The spirit was near complete eradication as Arima handed the roach clip to Jessie and said, "Hey, Jess. Wanna do the final honors?" Jessie looked at her friend and flashed her a devilish grin as she eagerly took the clip, lit the final remnants, and inhaled deeply. Arima heard one final anguished wail, leaned back on Marcus's chest, and smiled with deep satisfaction.

Following the most mellow, slow, and giggly house cleaning in the history of the world, there was a knock at the door. "Ah, they are here to remove the body," Louise stated as she floated towards the door. She opened it and gasped. "M-Mother Rhea! I was not expecting you! To what do we owe this honor?"

"Hello, Louise. It is so nice to see you again," the ninety-year-old Black woman stated as she was being supported by two other young women with a third directly behind them. "Well," Rhea continued while chuckling. "Perhaps 'see' isn't quite the right word. No, my eyes have never been able to see since I was born. But what my eyes can't see, my soul can. I can see people through their souls. I can tell whether a soul is filled with light or if it is filled with darkness. And I can see the potential that other women may possess. I can see their special gifts. I can see their power. And, since I failed your daughter so many years ago, Louise, I have vowed to not fail you again. So, it is time for me to meet your granddaughter. It is time for me to see *her*. It is time for me to see what this world has in store for her and what she has in store for it. So, may I please rest my weary bones and look upon this blessed child?"

"B-but of course, Mother Rhea! Please, won't you come in?" The young Black women, all in their late-teens escorted Rhea to a flowered chair. She placed her backside down and gave out an immediate yelp. "What is *this*, then?" she playfully asked as she reached under her rump and pulled out a cat claw. "Oh, my, you have a cat. Ah, yes, I see her there. So sweet. So protective. She will be of use to our cause."

As if on cue, LucyFur pounced upon Rhea's lap and began kneading her abdomen while purring. Rhea let out a delighted laugh as she pet the loveable feline before beginning. "Yes, as you know, Louise, I do not venture far from home much anymore. But there is a storm brewing. I can feel it. What we have experienced up to now is *nothing* compared to what we will all be confronted with in the coming years. There will be a period of relative calm before all hell breaks loose around us. It will be a hellacious battle upon this earth, and it will be a hellacious battle in the heavens. And these battles will be waged simultaneously. And we must all be prepared to play our part in this battle. All of us. Including your precious Arima. Come, dear. Come closer and take my hands. Let me look upon you."

"Ummm...okay," Arima calmly replied as she sauntered over to Rhea and took her hands. Rhea looked directly at Arima, and her milky-white eyes began weeping. After a few moments, Rhea composed herself and said, "Oh, my child. I knew that you would come one day, and I am so grateful that you have come in the form of an Azar. Your family has such a rich history. But you, my dear, are the most powerful one yet. I know that your grandmother wishes to protect you, but I am sorry. You cannot be protected. You are destined for greatness. Your hideous father knows this all too well. That is why he has tried to corrupt you. But he couldn't. You are too strong. Too powerful. And, you have too much of your mother's kindness in you. So now, he will try to destroy you. He *must* destroy you before you meet your... well...perhaps *that* is for another time.

"We must begin this by finding Arima's father and destroying him before he can destroy her." Rhea then looked up at the three identical women standing to the side of her chair. "My beautiful granddaughters have been searching for him. My darlings, Gwen, Rachel, and Kayla have the ability to track and locate souls. Especially demonic ones. But he is being hidden. His black soul is being cloaked by the power of his demonic overlord, Vetis. And there is another demon in the spirit realm that is assisting him. All that I can sense about her is that she is powerful, but not as powerful as she has been led to believe. She appears to me in a dark purple smog with a head of..."

"Copper!" Louise gasped out.

"Yes, copper," Rhea affirmed. "It is the copper one and Arima's damned father who are trying to keep Arima from engaging in this battle. They are trying to keep her away from...well...that won't happen for some time, so there's no point in speaking of it now."

"Speak about *what*?" Arima and Louise blurted out in unison. "C'mon Rhea," Arima began pleading. "What are you talking about? I have been through a lot of weird and painful shit for the past few months. I deserve to know everything. Plus, you tell me that I have to be prepared. So how am I supposed to be prepared if you're keeping secrets from me? C'mon, just tell me...*please?*"

"Oh, very well," Rhea conceded as Louise experienced a feeling of dread over what might be about to be revealed. "I actually do not know too much about this other one. She is nothing more than a sensation that I feel from time to time in my dreams. I do not know who she is or where she is or what she looks like, but what I *do* know is that she shouldn't exist. At least not as she is. She is the offspring of pure evil. She is the offspring of your father and another demon. Perhaps the copperhead, but I am not sure about that. She *also* should be pure evil. She should be waging war at her father's side and oppressing the downtrodden and brainwashing the gullible. But she isn't. Somehow, she has eluded his grasp. And somehow, she has become a great force against the very evil that spawned her. I can feel...I can *sense*...that there will come a time when she will need you, Arima. I can sense that there will be a time that you will be called to help her. That there will be a time that you are called to help your...half-sister."

Arima and Louise looked at one another in astonishment as Rhea continued. "But now is not the time to dwell upon that. It will do you no good to look for her. She is a needle in a million haystacks. She will reveal herself to you at the appropriate time. And when that time comes, I sense that the two of you will combine your great gifts and be most powerful. That is what I feel. That is what I sense. But on the other hand, what do I know? I'm just an old woman with too much time on my arthritic hands. So don't dwell on that now. What we must focus on is finding your father. We must find him so that you can destroy him. So that you can destroy him in both human and then spirit form. That must be our focus."

"But, Grandmother," Gwen, who was the leader of the Triplets, interjected. "We have tried. Even with our combined energy, we have not been able to locate him. We don't have a clue as to his whereabouts. How are we to find him?"

"I know, my darlings, I know," Rhea gently replied as she shook her head in frustration. "You three are such powerful hunters and yet this one has eluded you. Even with your combined might, you are unable to break through the defenses of Vetis. We must find someone who has an even *greater* gift than yours, my lovelies. We must find someone who has the gift to behold. The gift to behold both beauty and to behold great ugliness. This isn't a task for a tracker. This is a task for a Beholder and that, my dears, is simply something that you are not able to do."

Rhea's head then lifted, and her pure white eyes stared at the couch. She smiled and subtly nodded toward Jessie as she said eerily, "But *she* can".

Chapter 17

The Pitfalls of Peer Pressure

It had been two years since Jessie and Cliff had been home. They, along with Rachel, Gwen, Kayla, and…LucyFur, had been traveling the backroads of several southern states in an RV, searching for Arima's father. It was believed that Jessie's abilities as a Beholder would enhance the Triplets' ability to hone their soul tracking in on the slippery Pastor. Jessie had the ability to feel or behold pure good or pure evil in people, regardless of whether that evil was being cloaked. She could determine the general direction the feeling was coming from, leaving the Trackers to focus their energies on the specific dark soul that they were looking for. As the months went by, Jessie was amazed at how rapidly her newfound ability was developing. She was also amazed at the amount of pure evil that was present in the world. The feelings were overwhelming. The feelings made her painfully nauseous.

The first time that Jessie felt pure evil was in a small town in East Texas. Although the Trackers confirmed that the evil was not emanating from the specific dark soul that they were searching for, they stopped, nonetheless. They were compelled to stop as Jessie was in such anguish from the intensely unholy feelings that it was determined that the only way to relieve the pain was to eliminate the source of it. So they did. Mercilessly.

Cliff was in the bathroom of a shabby one-bedroom apartment vomiting as Rachel, Gwen, and Kayla stood over the body of a local child molester. There were disgusting pictures and trophies from his victims haphazardly hanging from the walls and lying on cluttered shelves. The television was playing a VHS tape that no one should ever witness, let alone experience. As the shrieks from young children screamed out of the television's speaker, the Triplets watched the man's blood flow from his slashed throat and begin to congeal around their matching black boots.

Jessie bound into the apartment holding a purring LucyFur. "Oh, man, I feel great!" she exclaimed. "What did you guys *do*? I was curled up in pain on the floor of the RV and then suddenly, it just stopped. All of the pain, like, just went away. And not only that, but I feel *rejuvenated*. Like this huge weight has been lifted off of me. I feel like I could just float into the clouds and…"

At that moment, the unobservant Jessie slipped in a pool of blood that had oozed toward the front door of the apartment. She fell backwards and landed solidly on her back as Cliff entered the room and yelled out to her. "Oh, my God, Jess! Are you all right?" Cliff exclaimed in a panicked voice as he rushed to his wife's side.

"Yeah, I'm okay," a slightly woozy Jessie replied as LucyFur began licking her face caringly. "What the hell *is* all of this? And, oh, my God! What did you guys *do*?"

Jessie sat up and saw the fresh corpse lying a few feet from her for the first time. Her bewildered brilliant blue eyes were wide open as Gwen replied.

"Well, y'know, we killed him. It was pretty easy. He answered the door, and we rushed him and pushed him back into his apartment. Kayla and I held his arms and Rachel slit his throat. And that was all there was to it. One more dick gone from the physical world. It's the only way, Jess. I talked to Grandmother last night and she said that once you have beheld pure evil, that it will hurt you, and that you won't be able to let go of it until the evil has been destroyed, so…y'know…we kinda did *this*. And it seemed to have worked. Are you upset?"

Jessie looked down at her blood-soaked dress as LucyFur began lapping up blood from around her. "Am I *upset*? Hell, *yes*, I'm upset! Look at my *dress*! Do you know how much this *cost*? And now it's *ruined*! How about a heads-up next time?"

That episode began a nearly two-year killing spree throughout Texas, Arkansas, and Oklahoma as the sextet traversed the highways and backroads searching earnestly for the Pastor. The regional news outlets dubbed the murderers the *Bayou Bloodletters*, which the Triplets found amusing. Cliff, on the other hand, did not.

Cliff had signed up for this mission for one reason and one reason only: to protect his cherished Jessie. His beloved wife had been attacked and the source of that attack was still at large. So, he would help in bringing down this demon. But he had not signed up for *this*. A week did not go by without the Triplets responding to Jessie's anguish with a brutal murder. And although he did not doubt the inherent evil of their victims, he also did not believe that they should be killed for it.

Cliff had been raised Catholic and was devout in his beliefs. He was incredibly popular in high school as he was the star quarterback on the football team. He was a kind soul who got along with all of the various cliques whether they be the goths, jocks, brains, or…stoners. He especially took a liking to one particular stoner of Jamaican descent and her best friend. They made him laugh. They helped him pass his classes through private tutoring. And they made him re-think some of what had been indoctrinated into him.

Although people like his new friends, Arima and Jamie, were proclaimed to be "sinners," with Arima's drug use and reputation for usually being up for a good time in someone's backseat and Jamie's flamboyance and flaunting of her transexual sexuality, he knew in his heart that they were good people. These were not people to be hated. They were nice and fun and generally non-judgmental. They did not believe all that *he* believed in, and he did not believe in everything that *they* did. And that was all right with him. That did not prevent the trio from enjoying going to the movies or out to dinner or bowling together. That did not prevent them from laughing together. That did not prevent them from crying together. And the three of them formed an unlikely bond of friendship.

A fourth member of this improbable group was added on the first day of football practice in August 2027. The sixteen-year old star hunched several feet behind the center and shouted out the cadence. The ball was snapped and at that moment, Cliff was blinded by a vision more beautiful than anything he had ever seen. Strutting across the field in her brand-new cheerleader outfit was a golden-haired, blue-eyed dream. The ball hit him in the facemask. Then what seemed to be the entire defensive unit hit him.

The impossible weight of the defensive players rolled off of him as the coach screamed at them in the background. He looked up and plummeted into two pools of intoxicating blue eyes. He smiled meekly as he awaited her expression of concern. And he received it.

The new transfer student, Jessie, scrunched up her petite nose and said forcefully, "*Wow*! If you play like that in a *real* game, then *I'm* not gonna have much to cheer about. And if I don't have much to *cheer* about, then the newspaper isn't going to take *my* picture. And if I don't get *publicity*, then I'm not going to attract *followers* to influence! So, how 'bout you get your shit together, huh, champ?"

As he watched her perfectly petite frame bounce back to her squad, he vowed that one day he would marry her. Which, as it turned out, was the only way that Jessie was going to get any action from him. As a devout Catholic, Cliff had sworn off of any sort of overly amorous pursuits until his wedding night. This was *not* an oath that Jessie was fond of, and she was continuously frustrated by nothing more than light petting and kissing. Jessie would consult with her new friends, Arima and Jamie, about how to get her beau into bed. Their reply was always the same. Marry him. This was always followed by loud guffawing at the sincere young man's expense.

Although frustrated by his rejection of her frequent enticements, Jessie grew to love her boyfriend, in her own self-serving way. He was sweet and kind. He was devastatingly handsome. And most importantly, he was loyal. Plus, it didn't hurt her reputation that the head cheerleader was seen dating the captain of the football team. She just wished that there was more accuracy in her title of head cheerleader.

During his senior season, Cliff proposed to Jessie in the middle of the football field following yet another victory. The team was to go to the playoffs. Jessie had been accepted at Tulane, which was where her boyfriend had received a scholarship, although certainly not for his academic prowess. The pair would be married following their freshman year. And then, all of Jessie's dreams would come true. She would be married to a high-profile future pro athlete. She would be a high-profile influencer. There would be money and houses and cars and gala events and shoes and shoes and shoes and fame. And finally, there would be sex. And maybe kids, who knows, we'll see.

All of those dreams came crashing down in the second quarter of the state championship game. Cliff dropped back to pass, trailing by three points. He spotted an open receiver jetting toward the corner of the end zone. He pulled back his arm to launch the ball and was viciously hit by a defender. He fell awkwardly onto his shoulder and ruptured his rotator cuff. The entire crowd gasped as they watched the medical cart pull onto the field toward the writhing young gladiator. Cliff's football career had come to a shattering end. Jessie's dreams had come to a shattering end.

There was a picture of Jessie in the next morning's newspaper. Her hands were clenched around her shocked pretty face. There were tears welling in her deep blues eyes. The photograph was the perfect representation of great loss, caring, and sweetness and the picture went viral. Well-wishers from all over the world began frequenting her social media platforms. From the ashes of Cliff's future rose Jessie, the Influencer.

But that was not the only thing that had been born for Jessie on that fateful evening. For the first time in her life, as she watched her fiancé screaming in pain, she felt something for someone other than herself. She was not crying because she believed that her dreams had just been vanquished. She was crying because she actually cared about the man that she had committed herself to. She realized at that tragic moment that she was completely and totally in love with her Cliff, and she vowed that she would follow through with their wedding. Enthusiastically. And soon.

That evening, Jessie crept into Cliff's private hospital room. She was wearing a short nurse's outfit. She gently laid on top of him and kissed him. She professed her love for him. And they made plans to wed the next April when both of them would be eighteen. He smiled and cried genuine tears of joy. There was a slight crumpling sound as the nurse's outfit fell to the cold linoleum floor. No one ever determined what Jesus Christ felt about the couple's passionate exploits that evening, but Cliff finally had something interesting to confess.

Cliff smiled to himself as he thought about the last seven years with his Jessie. Unable to play football and not having the exact academic qualities that colleges were looking for, Cliff worked as a laborer directly out of high school. He became quite skilled at building and could fix almost anything. He worked on construction sites and freelanced to build decks, remodel rooms, pour driveways or landscape. He had a well-earned reputation as an honest, hardworking young man and he was in constant demand. Cliff had never been ambitious. He just wanted to make enough money to keep his Jessie happy.

Unfortunately for Cliff, Jessie's spending habits were slightly more upscale than what he could afford. Especially when it came to shoes...and dresses...and jackets...and purses. Fortunately for him, however, Jessie had embarked on her own career as a successful and somewhat sought after influencer. She posted multiple times a day to turn her followers on to a new restaurant, perfume, vacation spot, exercise fad or, on some occasions, "massagers."

They moved in with Jamie shortly after they wed. Arima would join their household three years later, although nobody could really tell the difference as Arima was typically passed out on the couch most mornings as they were getting ready for work. They would look down at her crumb-encased frame and chuckle as they quietly would shut and lock the front door.

Cliff and Jessie weren't wealthy, but they were comfortable. And they were happy. Cliff never feared anything from Jessie, and he never feared *for* her. After all, he was always there to protect her. Until the night of the attack. And then, the revelation of her abilities as a Beholder which led to episodes of excruciating pain for her. Cliff felt helpless. He wanted so badly to be able to protect his beloved wife once again, but did not know how. He witnessed what killing the dark souls did for his wife but lamented the fact that the Triplets never tried anything else. He vowed that the next time Jessie had one of her episodes that he would talk the Triplets into capturing the evil-doer and taking them to the police for whatever dastardly deeds they were responsible for. He could not bear to be a witness to this bloodshed any longer. Not without trying something more humane, at least.

Then he thought about their mission. After two months on the road, it had become obvious to them that the Pastor was moving around and able to stay just out of their reach. As soon as Jessie felt his unique sensation of evil, it would dissipate. They knew that it was him. They knew that he could somehow sense that they were coming. They knew that he was on the run from them. And his elusiveness increased the frustration of the entire group with each passing day. But, although they had not cornered or captured him so that he may experience Arima's final judgement, they were successful in keeping him from implementing any sadistic plans through the indoctrination of a newly brainwashed congregation. He was simply too busy fleeing and trying to stay alive to focus on the bidding of Vetis.

Let's just get back to New Orleans without another one of Jess's episodes, Cliff thought to himself. *Lord, it will be so nice to see Arima and Jamie and everyone else again. It will be so nice to get a reprieve from this awful killing. It will be so nice to be normal again.*

At that moment, Jessie began shrieking and doubled over in pain. "Where is it, Jess?" Gwen shouted out. "Go that way!" Jessie yelled back through her gritted teeth. "Yes, that way! It's getting stronger!"

The RV pulled next to a barn. The Triplets poured out of the RV and opened the barn doors. There, they found fourteen corpses hanging from meat hooks. All of the corpses were non-white, and their blood was dripping off of them and pooling on the floor. They were all in various stages of dismemberment or disembowelment. The stench of the rotting flesh nearly bowled the young women over. They didn't believe that the scene could be any more gruesome. They were wrong. They looked to their right and saw the meat grinder.

A dark silhouette ran out of the back entrance of the barn. The Triplets unsheathed their knives and followed. Cliff was sitting in the driver's seat preparing for a fast getaway with the hopefully captured and not killed evil-doer. He saw the dark silhouette from the rear-view mirror. It was approaching the RV with the Triplets following. Jessie was sobbing on the floor of the RV constricted in pain. He looked at his wife and his heart was pounding. He looked at the fast-approaching silhouette and his heart pounded faster. He acted. He sprung from the driver's seat and opened the side panel door of the RV just as the silhouette was about to pass. He tackled the man sending a sharp pain through his previously repaired rotator cuff. He picked the man up by his shaved head and placed him on his knees.

"Please, Cliff, do something! He's too close! I can't stand the pain!" Jessie cried out.

He looked once again at his tortured wife and his heart pounded. He looked into the barn and saw the hanging bodies and his heart pounded faster. He looked at the three ominous black-clad women surrounding him with their knives drawn. They slowly nodded at him in unison. He drew in a deep breath and his heartbeat relaxed as he snapped the man's neck.

"Oh, my God, that was worse than the others. Thank you, baby. Thank you for taking care of him," a tearful Jessie cried out as she threw herself around his neck, sobbing.

"You're welcome, baby. It's okay. I'll never let anybody hurt you again. I don't care *what* I have to do. Nobody will *ever* hurt you again."

He looked at the wry smiles on the faces of Rachel, Gwen, and Kayla and said softly, "C'mon. Let's get back on the road. We have an engagement party to get to."

Chapter 18

Dead Beat Dads

As Marcus walked toward Clyde's office, he was smiling at the thought of the most romantic conversation that he had ever had just a few weeks prior. As he and Arima were lying in her bed surrounded by the crumbs and wrapper remnants of their most recent gluttonous orgy, Marcus said nonchalantly, "So, we've been goin' out now for around two years".

"Uh, huh," Arima replied followed by a soft belch.

"Well," Marcus continued, "You wanna maybe get married or something?"

"Yeah, sure," came Arima's reserved response. "Why not? We get along okay, and we have similar interests and…hey do you want the last bite of this pizza?"

"Naw, you can have it," Marcus answered. "So, when do ya wanna get married?"

"I dunno," Arima replied with her mouth full of pizza crust and marinara dipping sauce dripping down her chin. "How about in a couple years? Knowing us, it'll take us that long to figure out what we want to do. Cool?"

"Yeah, cool," Marcus answered before asking, "So I suppose you'll want a ring, right?"

"Yeah, that would be nice, I guess," Arima replied before concluding with, "And a party. This will be a good excuse to have a party and get Cliff and Jess back here for a while."

Marcus wiped a tear from his overjoyed eyes and entered Clyde's office.

"Marcus!" Clyde enthusiastically exclaimed. "Come in, my lad, come in! You're here a bit early for your shift. What is it that I can do for you? Oh, I know. It *has* been a while since your last raise, hasn't it? Well, son, the budget is a bit tight right now, but you do such a *wonderful* job. I'll tell you what I'll do. I'll speak with some of the muckety-mucks and see if I can't squeeze out another twenty-five cents an hour, hmmm? Will that keep you in our happy little family?"

"Uh, yeah, thanks," Marcus awkwardly replied. "Yeah, that would be great, but that's not really why I'm here. You see, Arima and I just got engaged and we're throwing this party and, well, I was just wondering if you knew where I could get a nice suit for…y'know…kinda cheap."

Clyde squealed in delight in response. "Engaged? To Arima? Oh, how exciting! We haven't had such exciting news around here since the Peterson family deaths of '27! Oh, that was a sad sight. Speaking of which, do you have an engagement ring yet?"

"Uh, no," Marcus answered. "That was another question I was gonna ask you".

Clyde bounced from his creaky and worn office chair and said excitedly, "Come, come, come my lad. I have a little something to show you." Marcus followed Clyde down the hallway. He unlocked a heavy metal door and they entered another hallway. Marcus got chills as the temperature seemed to plummet in the dark corridor. They approached another metal door and Clyde looked up at Marcus with the flashlight lit under his face wearing a macabre smile.

Marcus shuddered as Clyde said in a cartoonish, dark tone, "Spoooooky isn't it? MWAHAHAHAHAAAA!" Seeing the shocked look on Marcus's face, Clyde quickly retreated. "Oh, my lad, I'm so sorry. I didn't mean to frighten you. You know how I love my little jokes. Here, step inside and feast your eyes upon this!"

Clyde opened the door and turned on the light. The overhead neon began flickering and buzzing as Marcus saw a large room filled with clothing. There were dresses and suits and casual wear all organized and hung neatly on racks.

Marcus had a sinking feeling as he asked the question that he was afraid to hear the answer to. "Wh-wh-what the hell *is* all of this, Clyde?"

"Oh, just my little stockpile, hee, hee, hee," Clyde gleefully responded.

"You see, oftentimes our guests' clothing has been...um...stained or damaged in some way and their family does not want to keep them. So I have them cleaned and repaired as best I can, and I store them here for just such an occasion! Where do you think that I get all of *my* fine clothes?"

Marcus looked at Clyde's light blue shirt and noticed the slight red stain on the chest and felt nauseous. "Now, let's just find your size," Clyde continued as he pranced to a rack in the middle of the room. "Oh, my. We have some fine options for you here. Lucky for you, most of the connected men in the city are a bit...well...big-boned. Yes, those men do like to eat. And their fashion sense is impeccable! Look at these designer brands. You just need to overlook the few bullet holes and they are absolutely perfect! Here's one! Come, come! Try it on! I'll look for some shoes! You look to be size...hmmm...Arima is a lucky girl."

Marcus hesitantly took the suit and went into a small closet, disrobed and put the "new" suit on. *Awww damn, this is creepy. I don't wanna wear some dead dude's clothes. I'll have to find a way to let Clyde down easy,* Marcus thought to himself as he zipped up his slacks and tucked in the white shirt that had a few brownish-red embellishments around repaired holes. He looked at himself in the mirror and then thought, *Awww damn! I look sharp! Arima's gonna be all over me in this!*

Marcus emerged and Clyde squealed in delight once again as he looked upon this tall, handsome man whose somewhat portly features were concealed by a light grey with dark grey pinstripe double-breasted suit. The white shirt gleamed behind the designer silver tie. Clyde smiled up at him and handed Marcus a pair of black socks and shiny black Italian boots. Marcus beamed and quickly accepted the generous offering.

"Now for the ring," Clyde snickered as he opened a drawer and dug deep under a cornucopia of women's delicates. "Aw, here it is. We, of course, do not...um...inherit very many valuables. The family always takes those. But this ring was never claimed. And it is absolutely stunning!"

Clyde handed the ring to Marcus who marveled at it. The center diamond was at least three karats and fit inside a wedding band that wrapped around it in a diamond-encrusted orbit. "Clyde," Marcus began stammering. "I, I can't afford anything like this. I mean, it's absolutely beautiful, but I just can't swing it. Thanks for showing it to me, though."

"Afford?" Clyde gasped in response. "Why, my lad, who said anything about *money*? No, you may have this. It's not like I can sell it or pawn it. I just kept it here for safekeeping, hoping some lovely couple might cherish it as much as its original owner did. Yes, this was what gave me the idea to bring you in here. This ring belonged to Becky Peterson. It was said that she was a sweet young woman. She had two lovely little daughters. And she had a husband. One night, when their girls were around five and three, Mr. Peterson was away on business. There was a gas leak in the home and Becky and her darling daughters all asphyxiated. It was so sad and tragic. The husband was so remorseful that he didn't want to keep the ring. He just couldn't bear the sight of any reminders of his lost love. So this delightful little item has been sitting here for the past nine years waiting. Waiting for someone to come along and cherish it. It has been waiting for you and Arima. Please take it, my lad. Take it and put a wonderful smile on Arima's face. All that I ask in return is that…well…perhaps I could be invited to your little gathering?"

Marcus screamed in delight, picked Clyde up, and spun him around. Clyde's combed-over, greasy black hair looked like streamers on a kite as they flew in the breeze. "Okay, okay, put me down, now," Clyde stated through his giggles. "And one more thing. Well, this is such good news. Perhaps I can squeeze a bit *more* out of those muckety-mucks for both you *and* Arima."

Jamie clasped her hands over her mouth and let out a high-pitched shriek as Arima walked into her bedroom wearing a traditional Jamaican dress that was covered in yellow and green hibiscus flowers. Jamie's tears began flowing as she embraced her best friend on the evening of Arima's engagement party.

Jamie was overcome with joy. Arima was not only her best friend. Arima was her savior. Arima was her hero. From the time they had met in junior high, Arima was the one person that Jamie could tell her secrets to. All of them. When she told Arima in eighth grade that, although she was born a boy, she felt as though she was a girl, Arima's response was, "Yeah, alright. So, you gonna finish that last cookie or what?"

"You mean you don't care?" an astonished Jamie inquired of her best friend and confidant.

"Well, yes and no," Arima replied casually. "I mean, on the one hand, I personally don't care at all. I mean, why would I? We're all made different. You were born a boy and you like boys, but you feel like you're a girl. Okay. What the hell do I care? All I know is that you're Jamie. You're my friend. You're kind and sweet and smart and I love you. What more do I need to know?"

"On the other hand, I care a lot. I care that other people care so much about something that there's nothing to care about. No...wait. They don't *care* so much as they *hate* other people just for being who they are. Whether it's a trans person, or a Black person, or a woman, or...hey. I just thought of something. Man, you are so *screwed*. You are a Black young man who wants to be with other young men and who wants to be a woman. Man, all of the fascist religious freaks are going to come after *your* ass. And not in the good way. That's why I care. I care because there are hateful people in our world who hate you just for who you are. You could be the nicest person in the world. You could save them from death, and they would still hate you. So I personally don't give a shit, but I *do* care about how many people are going to hate you for it. And I'll tell you this much. I will never leave you, no matter what, okay?"

Jamie had tears flowing from her eyes as she embraced her best friend. Several years later, Jamie decided that she was tired of hiding who she truly was and began wearing women's clothing. But only in her bedroom. When she was sixteen, she was standing in her bedroom looking in the mirror at her beautiful reflection. She looked dazzling in full makeup, silver hoop earrings, a short afro, and a glistening silver gown that she had found at a secondhand shop. She turned and twirled and posed and giggled as she looked at herself from every angle. For the first time in her life, she felt like herself. For the first time in her life, she saw Jamie.

Her father approached her bedroom door wishing to speak to his son, James. He opened the door and discovered that he had a daughter named Jamie. "I knew you were a goddamn fruit!" her father bellowed as he removed the belt from around his waist. Jamie screamed in physical, emotional, and mental agony as her father beat her. And beat her. And beat her. And beat her. The last words that she ever heard her father say were, "Get the hell out of my house and never come back, you freak. I have no son. And I sure as hell don't have a daughter."

Jamie limped the two miles to Arima's house through back alleys so as not to be discovered by the local hoodlums, racists, and homophobes. She meekly knocked upon Arima's door. Louise Azar answered the door and took one look at the tragic sight that stood before her. Jamie's lips were split open. Both eyes were battered and swelling. Black mascara and bright blue eye shadow streamed down her bruised face. Her silver gown was tattered and did nothing to cover the multiple purple welts that were forming upon her back, legs and chest.

Louise opened her arms and embraced Jamie's beaten body. Louise opened her heart and embraced Jamie's beaten soul. And Louise opened her home and embraced Jamie with the love, understanding, respect, and support that she so richly deserved. Jamie spent the rest of the night lying in Arima's caring embrace as both friends wept uncontrollably. And Jamie and Arima had never left each other's side from that tragically joyful moment on.

Jamie wiped the celebratory tears from her eyes and said with an apologetic laugh, "Oh, my darling, heh…I may have gotten some makeup on your lovely dress."

"Well," Arima softly replied. "It wouldn't be the first time and I'm sure it won't be the last. C'mon, I think our guests are arriving."

The pair went downstairs and let out an exuberant shriek as they saw their best friends, Jessie and Cliff, for the first time in nearly two years. LucyFur purred as she circled Arima's ankles as the quartet embraced. The Triplets made themselves drinks and began discussing their findings, or lack thereof, to Louise, who sat pensively and nodded. Clyde arrived with a bouquet of flowers and several bottles of alcohol.

"Clyde!" Arima exclaimed as she hugged her boss. "Thanks so much for coming! What's with all the booze?"

"Oh, well," Clyde responded mischievously. "What I hold here, my dear, is all of the ingredients for my specialty drink. So would you like me to make you a zombie? Heh, heh, heh."

The entire group jumped with a start as they heard a high-pitched squeal from Jamie. They then relaxed as they saw the sharp-dressed, lumbering, hairy reasons for the shriek. "Stellan! Paciano! You made it! Oh, come here, my lovelies!"

The entire room was in awe as they listened to Stellan and Paciano's exploits from the past two years. They told everybody how excited they were because they may get to move back to their home county. The group recoiled as they spoke about how they, and many others, had been driven from their homes by the local fascists. The beatings. The rapes. The murders. Anyone who did not succumb to their White Christian nationalist rule was a victim of it. The silver-haired Stellan's cadence became excited, however, when he began speaking about how a group of freedom fighters from Brooklyn had begun beating back the fascists. "And *these* are people," the black-dyed-haired Paciano interjected, "that are good to know. They are *brutal* in what they do. But no more brutal than what the fascists have been doing to all of us. It's just that what *they* do is beat down those that are beating down the innocent. The oppressed. We have heard such amazing stories of their exploits. They primarily work to keep the fascists and other undesirables out of Brooklyn, but we have heard that they have done things internationally as well. *We*, of course, aren't involved with *them*, but…"

Paciano was then cut off by Stellan. "That we *know* of. There are rumors, but nobody outside of their little group *really* knows who they are. Oh, darling! Remember that rumor about the cute little family who may hire us to care for their estate in our county once it is cleared of fascists? Oh, my, how hysterical! That is how *crazy* some of these rumors are. To think that such a cute little hum-drum family with the most *adorable* copper-headed little twelve-year-old girl could be involved with such…brutality. Well, we all had a big laugh over that one!"

Louise's spine stiffened upon hearing this last sentence. She shot a look at her beloved granddaughter who looked back and just rolled her eyes and shrugged. The tension was immediately broken between the two as the front door opened once again. Marcus and his proud parents entered the living room and were greeted immediately with joyful embraces.

Marcus looked at Arima in her smart hibiscus Jamaican dress. Arima looked at Marcus in his grey pinstripe double-breasted suit. They stared at each other for thirty seconds before Arima grabbed Marcus by the hand and said, "Come on!" The pair returned downstairs to their party eighteen minutes later, wearing lasciviously ornery smiles.

The revelry of drinks, food, stories and laughter flowed nonstop until everyone noticed Marcus take Arima by the hand and lead her to the center of the living room. He looked at her and smiled sheepishly as he said, "Well, I know I've already asked you this, but…um…well…I, like, got a ring, so I thought maybe we could make it official."

Although Arima already knew what he was about to ask, again, she couldn't keep her heart from beating through her chest. She watched in anticipation as Marcus went to one knee, looked up at her with tears forming in his eyes, and said, "Arima, will you marry me?"

This was a moment that would become one of Arima's most cherished memories. She did not want to mess this moment up. Arima messed the moment up.

"Uh, yeah, well, *maaaaybe*, heh, heh, heh," she replied mischievously.

"Arima!" Louise bellowed out. "You say, 'yes' this moment, young lady!"

"Fine! Whatevs. Just tryin' to be funny. Y'know...lighten the mood a little? Jeez! Fine! Yes, I will marry you!"

The entire room burst into laughter and tears as Marcus placed the extravagantly elegant ring upon Arima's finger. "What the *hell*, dude?" Arima cried out upon seeing the impossibly large engagement ring. "You win the lottery or something?"

"Naw," Marcus replied modestly as he looked over at a prideful Clyde. "I just had a little help, that's all. I hope you like it."

"Like it?" Arima cried out. "I love it! It's the most beautiful thing that..."

Arima stopped her sentence abruptly as she heard a voice say through her soul, *Who the hell are you that's wearing my ring?*

"Um...Marcus?" a concerned Arima whispered. "Where the hell did you get this ring?"

"Uh...listen, everybody," Arima then stated to her guests. "Listen, it's been a helluva night. It's been so great. I just need to go for a walk with my...y'know...fiancé and cool down a bit, okay? Just keep the party going. Oh, and you've got to try those brownies. I made them myself with my secret herb recipe. They'll knock you on your ass! Okay, we'll be back in a bit."

As the pair walked down the sidewalk, Arima said to Marcus, "Okay, I don't know where you got this ring, but there's a spirit in here, so if I'm gonna wear this, I need to get her outta here. I don't really want to walk around with spirits on my finger 'til death do us part, okay?"

"Yeah, okay," Marcus replied flatly. "So what else is new? I knew I shouldn't have used a ring from the morgue."

"The...*what?*" a shocked Arima yelled out. "The *morgue?* You got it from the *morgue?* Okay, we'll deal with that later. I've gotta straighten this shit out. Okay, spirit. You've got my attention. Just tell me how we can work this out, okay?"

All right, Arima, the spirit spoke to her. *I'm sorry to have frightened you. It really is so nice to be connected with you. And I think it's lovely that you are wearing my ring. You two make such a lovely couple. But I cannot move on, Arima. Not without your help. Will you help me? Will you help us?*

"Us? Who else is in there with you?" Marcus heard Arima say to no one.

My daughters, Arima. My daughters, the spirit replied. *My name is Becky Peterson. We died in 2027. There was a gas leak in our house. It was ruled an accident. But it wasn't. My husband and their father...murdered us. Oh, he thought he was so clever. The fake alibi. The award-winning acting. Oh, he was so smooth as he played the part of the grieving husband and father. No one suspected him. But it was him. I saw him do it. I saw him sneak back into our house after saying he would be away on business. I saw him sabotage the gas line. He grabbed me and put something over my mouth. That was my final living memory. He murdered me and his two daughters. My lord, Arima, they were only five and three at the time.*

Arima then heard two more voices. They were the voices of innocent little girls that said, *Our daddy is a bad man. He hurt us. Can you help us? Mommy says that there's a playground in the sky. Can you help us find it?*

So, Arima, Becky's voice began once again. *What will it be? Will you help us? Or are you going to wear trapped spirits on your left hand for the rest of your life?*

"Okay, I'll help you," Arima replied with resignation. "But it's gotta be quick. I gotta get back to my party before they eat all of the brownies. But before we do whatever it is that you need me to do, tell me one thing. Why did he do it?"

Oh, Arima, Becky responded with a sigh. *Why do brutal men do anything? Power? Money? Sex? I don't know. He was a sociopath, I suppose, and just got off on it. He got off on holding our lives in his hands and then destroying us. And don't worry about your party. We will get you back real soon. I know just where he is. Let us take over your body. We will take care of the rest.*

Becky Peterson used Arima's body to climb onto the deck of the yacht. Arima could see and feel everything as Becky scanned the deck. She found what she was looking for. She picked the fisherman's knife up and descended the stairs to the main cabin. There he was. Half-drunk with yet another drink in his hand.

Girls, you know what to do, was all that Arima heard before her body pounced upon the shocked man.

"Hi Daddy! We're back!" one of the girls cried out as Arima's right hand began plunging the knife into the gasping man's chest. "Yes, we're back! Die

Daddy! Die Daddy! Die Daddy"! The three-year-old spirit repeated as she punctured the screaming man over and over again.

Blood was spraying throughout the cabin and all over Arima's dress as Marcus looked on with quiet reservation. He looked down at his watch and said calmly, "Listen. We've been gone nearly two hours. We need to get back. I know this is your big moment and everything, but what else is there to do?"

"Oh, there's one more thing to do," a sinister voice rolled off of Arima's tongue. "Now, it's *my* turn girls!" The dying man could do nothing but gurgle and spit up frothy blood as Becky used Arima's body to meticulously saw the man's head off with the serrated knife. Arima's body was cackling in three different pitches as she placed the head in the microwave and pressed *'High'*. Arima's body then sat on the adjacent sofa and watched the microwave intensely until she heard a loud 'pop.'

Marcus watched as three blue streaks of light floated majestically out of Arima's body. *Thank you, Arima. Perhaps there will be a time when we can help you. Enjoy my ring*, Becky stated sincerely.

Yes! Thank you, Arima! We're going to go play now! Oh, look, mommy! Look at how silly Daddy's head looks! It's all mushy and gooey like our play dough! Arima wiped a tear from her eye as the little girls' giggling voices faded away with their souls.

As the pair were preparing to leave the yacht, Marcus said, "Hey, aren't you forgetting something?"

"Uh, I don't think so, why?" Arima replied.

"Well, isn't that bad dude's spirit still hanging around here? Don't you think you should finish him off so he can't ever cause any more problems?" Marcus elaborated.

"Oh, yeah. Thanks for reminding me, baby," an appreciative Arima responded. "Now, where are you? It won't do you any good to hide from me. I've got like evil spirit radar and shit so, oh…there you are. C'mon in."

Arima extended her arms and elevated briefly off of the floor before returning back down. "Okay, I've got him. And, man, he's scared as shit. As well he should be. Damn murdering prick. And his own wife and kids, too. Sometimes I still get shocked at the level of evil some people are possessed with. Now, where should I put you?"

Marcus smiled and handed Arima a half-full bottle of rum, a rolled-up bar towel, and a lighter.

As Arima and Marcus were walking hand in hand off of the pier there was a tremendous explosion from behind them. They didn't bother to look back. They didn't even break their stride.

The entire group gasped as Arima and Marcus re-entered their home. "Uh, sorry. We just went for a snack," Arima tried to explain. "I guess I spilled some ketchup on your dress, Grams. Sorry."

"That's all right my dear. Accidents happen," a smirking Louise answered as she watched LucyFur begin to lick the "ketchup" from off of Arima's dress.

Chapter 19

Aloha

How was your engagement party, Arima? Mrs. Roper playfully inquired before making over-exaggerated kissing noises and laughing.

"Man," Arima replied, "You know what? I think the older that you two get, the more immature you get. The party was great. I'm still kinda hung over and it was two days ago. You happy now? Now, just grow up!"

Oh, what fun would that be, dear? a laughing Mr. Roper interjected. *If we have to be stuck in this godforsaken morgue, the least we can do is have a bit of fun. Besides, watching you and Marcus keeps us young. Oh, how we wish we could have been there to see the celebration.*

"Yeah, me too," Arima responded with a genuine tone of regret. "You guys have kinda become like parental figures to me. You've done so much for me. You've sacrificed for me. You have put off going to Enlightenment just to stay here and help me. But, as it turns out, there probably wasn't enough room in my soul to have brought you two along."

What do you mean, dear? Mrs. Roper inquired.

"Well," Arima began through a light chuckle and said with a hint of sarcasm, "My *romantic* fiancé went *all out* and got me a ring from the *morgue*. Which is okay, I guess, because it's *absolutely gorgeous*. It's just that…well…"

At that moment Mr. Roper looked at the ring for the first time. *Oh, my!* he exclaimed. *Why, that is the ring that Becky Peterson was wearing when she was brought in here. Oh, she was so protective of her darling little girls that she hid* them in that ring. And then, once the husband showed no interest in it, Clyde took it and locked it away. It must have been a dark existence for them. Were you able to help them, dear?*

"Yeah," Arima answered as she began sorting through that evening's paperwork to be filed. "It turns out her husband murdered them all, so, well, y'know. Her and her little girls used me to stab him, decapitate him and then put his head in the microwave to…well…kersplode it. Man, those little girls were…creepy as hell. But I guess being murdered by your father will do that to a spirit. Anyway, I took his dark soul, put it in a rum bottle with a rag for a fuse, lit it, and left that bastard to be blown up for all time. We did, however, leave a bit of a mess. Three other yachts in the marina got burned pretty badly. Oh well. It's not like those rich bastards don't have insurance. I guess they'll just have to rough it with their five vacation homes and two other yachts, heh, heh, heh. And maybe they won't have much money to buy off corrupt politicians, either. I saw where one of the yachts was owned by the CEO of a gun manufacturer. Man, I wish I could have the chance to mess up *his* greedy, rotten soul."

You know, dear, Mrs. Roper broke in. *I believe Clyde put our clothes from the night of our death back there.*

Yes, I believe you are right, Mr. Roper agreed.

"Hey! That gives me an idea!" Arima shouted out. "I think I know how you can make amends to your kids and then move on!"

No, Arima, Mr. Roper resisted, *We are needed here. We will go when the time is right.*

"The time *is* right," Arima argued back. "You two have been patient long enough. You have watched for the past two years as I've helped other trapped souls move on. You have patiently and selflessly helped me. Now it's *your* turn. I will always love you and I will miss you, but *now* is the time. Just listen. Do you think maybe *this* might work?"

The following morning, Clyde came into the morgue, whistling. "Goooood morning, Arima!" he exclaimed as he entered the room. "Oh, what a lovely party you two threw last Saturday! To watch two young lovers commit to one another. It…well…it warmed my heart. Thank you so much for inviting me. I had such a wonderful time meeting your family and friends."

"Yeah, you're welcome and thanks for coming. Those drinks you made were…um…strong," Arima replied. "Say, Clyde? Do you remember a couple named Roper?"

"Oh, yes," Clyde answered. "But they passed some time ago. Oh, what a sight! Those two got drunk and plowed head-on into a car of teenagers. And they left two young children behind. I don't say this often, but if there is a hell, then those two are certainly in it!"

Well, maybe it wouldn't be so much of a hell if you would put up some damned decorations! Arima could hear Mrs. Roper angrily declare. *And who are you to judge? You don't know us! You don't know all that we have done to…to…* Mrs. Roper ended her sentence as she broke down into tears.

"Yeah, um, so do you still have their clothes? Um, their kids called…yeah, that's it! Their kids called and wanted them back. I don't know why, but I figured that if we still have them that it wouldn't hurt anything to give them back. I guess they still live together. Neither one of them has ever really dated or gotten married or anything. Their daughter is twenty-one and their son is nineteen now. They just work and come home to each other. They're afraid to fall in love, I guess, so they've kinda shut down their hearts to it."

"I…see," a suspicious Clyde responded. "Tell me, Arima. Just how do you know all of this about their children?"

"Oh, just something that I heard from a little birdie. So, do you have the clothes?"

"Why, yes, I do! I will go retrieve them at once!" Clyde answered enthusiastically. "Can you call them and tell them that they're ready for pick-up?"

"Uh, actually," Arima replied, "I was going to just drop them off at their house, if that's okay."

The children of Mr. and Mrs. Roper opened their front door to leave their home for another day of office-based drudgery. They looked down and saw a large box that was wrapped in paper that had their favorite animated mouse on it from when they were children. They both wore perplexed expressions as they looked at one another. The sister picked up the box and re-entered their home with her younger brother directly behind her.

The Ropers looked on with anticipation through Arima's eyes as they peered through a living room window. They saw their beloved children carefully unwrap the package and open the box. They let out a gasp as they took out their mother's dress and their father's shirt and slacks from the evening of their deaths. They began crying as they retrieved an envelope from the bottom of the box and opened it with quiet trepidation.

The children's eyes widened as they looked upon the letter that was written first in their mother's hand, then their father's. Their widened eyes continued to weep as they put their heads together and silently read.

Mr. and Mrs. Roper were sobbing as well as they watched their children read what they had written to them.

Oh, our darlings. We are so sorry to shock you like this and we know that this is hard to believe, but this letter is truly from us, your deceased parents. These are the clothes that we were wearing on the night that we made so many mistakes. We wanted you to have them to remind you of the foolish mistakes that we made. Our selfishness and misguided jealousy led us to kill those four innocent teenagers. And it led us to leaving you. Leaving you without truly knowing us. Leaving you without giving you better guidance about how to be good, kind, loving people. We have been watching you and have chosen now to say hello...and good-bye one final time. Please know that the example that we set for you is not how relationships are supposed to work. We allowed ourselves to take each other for granted. We allowed ourselves to become bored with one another. This led us to selfish acts that were nothing more than a betrayal to one another. And then, the jealousy. And the anger. And the intentionally hurting one another. We were so stupid, my dears. We know that we have left you with callous hearts, but please know that we are not the example that you should follow. Please, my dears, allow yourself to open up your hearts to others. Please allow yourself to love and be loved. It doesn't always work out. There will be ups and downs. But there is nothing in this world like finding the one that you were meant to be with. I found that man. I had forgotten how much I loved him for a time. But I remember now. I remember who it was that I first fell in love with. And I am pleased to say that I will be with that man for all of eternity.

Yes, you will dear. And I am pleased to spend eternity with you as well. Hi, kids. This is your father. You know that I'm not really great with words, but I, too, want to tell you that your parents were stupid, silly people. Life is short and can be extinguished at any moment. I think that I have a bit of expertise on the subject. Take advantage of every moment of your life. Every breath. Find that special someone and share those moments with them. Laugh together. Cry together. Love together. Please let go of your bitterness and allow yourself to feel the joy of being cherished by another. Allow yourself the joy of cherishing someone else. Be honest with and trust that other person. But, most importantly, be kind to that other person and allow them to be kind to you. That's really all that it takes. I just wish that it hadn't taken this tragedy for us to learn that. We have to go now. We are moving on. But we will say hello to you each morning. Just look in the tree in your front yard. You will see two birds chirping. That will be us saying that we love you.

The brother and sister carefully folded the letter and placed it back into the envelope. The envelope was placed back into the box and the clothes were delicately folded and placed back on top of the letter. They tenderly re-wrapped the package and placed it under their family portrait. It seemed to them that their parents' smiles were wider and more sincere. More loving. They laughed, wiped their tears from their eyes and embraced. "What do you say we skip work today?" the sister asked.

"Yeah, let's just enjoy our lives today. For Mom and Dad," the brother responded with sentimentality.

The Ropers continued to watch from the bushes as they saw their children leave the house together. There was a young man arriving across the street to tend to the landscaping. He saw the daughter, waved, and smiled. The daughter blushed, waved back and said, "Hey! We'll be back in a couple of hours! Why don't you come by after you're done working? I'll make you some lemonade!" The man smiled more widely and eagerly nodded.

A young woman then came jogging past their front yard. She flashed the son a flirtatious smile, then stopped. "Hey, I've seen you around before," she said playfully. "You know, I jog by here every morning trying to get your attention and you have not *once* even glanced at me. Listen, it's cool if I'm not your type or...y'know...gender. But I'm just gonna offer this once. You wanna go out sometime?"

"Uh...uh...uh," the son began stammering to his father's glee as he watched on. "S-sure. Um, do you wanna grab a bite to eat? Maybe tonight?"

The young woman chuckled and said, "Yeah, you're cute. I'll be by around six. See ya then!"

The pair of siblings looked at one another, laughed, and proceeded down the sidewalk.

They were unable to hear their mother's voice say, *Thank you, Arima. We can rest peacefully now.*

Yes, Mr. Roper added. *Thank you, my dear. We will love you always. We will love you as much as we love our own children.*

Arima felt the two souls detach and lift out of hers. She looked up at the sky at the two floating blue and white streaks of light. And she wept out of joyful loss.

"Aw, shit," she said aloud to herself. "I don't know how much of this I can take today. Now I gotta go to Grams and say good-bye to Jess and Cliff. Okay, baby, do your stuff," she concluded before lighting a fresh joint and inhaling deeply the intoxicating smoke from her own personally grown stash. "Wow!" she exclaimed. "Damn, Herbert. I don't know if you can hear me, but this stuff truly is amazing. Thanks again. This will help me get through my day."

As Arima turned to begin her walk to the bus stop, she did not notice the cluster of bright pink tulips that suddenly grew out of the ground and bloomed.

Arima opened the door and said flatly, "Hey, Grams," before looking up and seeing Rhea who was there to once again say good-bye to her granddaughters. And to do one other thing.

"Oh, my dear Jessie," Rhea was saying as Arima casually sauntered into the room and took a seat next to Cliff and Louise. "I know your gift has caused you such pain. I have known only one other Beholder in my time and she...well...wasn't terribly interested in using her gift. I truly did not know that it would be so hard on you my dear. I knew that there would be discomfort until you vanquished the evil that you were feeling, but I did not know just how debilitating that it would be. For the last two years, I have been trying to find some help for you. And I believe that I have. There is an ancient incantation that I have found. It was buried deep in one of my very old books and is reserved just for Beholders. Here is the incantation, my dear. When you behold true evil, you will still experience intense pain. But if a *pure* soul who is also a Beholder recites this incantation that pain can be transformed into...strength. Pure, unbridled, physical strength. You will have the strength of ten women combined and will have that strength for as long you are trying to vanquish the dark soul. Then, upon their death, you will return to normal. You'll be a bit tired, probably, but normal."

Arima burst out laughing and said through her herb-induced chortles, "Hey, Rhea! She has to be a *pure* soul? I've heard what she and Cliff do in their bedroom! There ain't *nothing* pure about *her* soul or anything else for that matter. I guess you two need to go back to strict missionary or you're screwed! And not in the good way!"

Jessie flashed her friend a look that could kill. Rhea shook her head in wonderment. Cliff blushed and looked towards the floor. Louise clasped her hand over her mouth in an attempt to not burst out laughing. And for the very first time, LucyFur growled at Arima.

"I mean," Arima immediately stated in an attempt to back-track, "I'm just, y'know, jokin'. That's really great news Jess. You'll be like a short-term superhero or somethin'. That's totally great and I just *know* it'll work on you because you are the *purest* soul I know…right, LucyFur?"

LucyFur stopped growling and pounced upon Arima's chest. Arima began sweating as the cat glared directly into her eyes. She then began kneading Arima's chest, laid down, and began purring.

Heh, heh, heh, came the sinister voice of Howard from the scenic Jamaican painting. *You had better not mess with that cat, girl. That cat has bonded with Jessie and will do anything to protect her. And I, Arima, will do anything to protect you. Really. When it comes time to battle your father, I want you to let me in. Let me help you again. I can help organize the others.*

"What others?" Arima said aloud to the perplexed looks of her friends.

The others, Arima. The other spirits that you have helped. They are connected to you. They are as protective of you as that demon cat is of Jessie. And they will be able to help you. They do not need to enter your body. Not any longer. They can now come to Earth and aid you directly while in spirit form. All that they need from you is a prayer for help. And they will be there. And I can help you organize an attack. And I want to say that I am not doing this just to get into Enlightenment and out of this damned painting. I am taking a risk, too. If you die while I'm in you, then I die, too. I'm truly not doing this for myself. I am offering this to help you. So, kid. What do ya say? Partners?

The entire room burst out laughing as Arima exclaimed for some unknown reason. "Fine! We'll give it a shot! But I'm gonna say this again! No pegging, and I mean it!"

You really aren't much fun, Howard replied with disappointment.

Chapter 20

Queen High Flush

August in East Texas had always been hot. But August in East Texas in the year 2037 was nearly unbearable with high temperatures consistently averaging near one-hundred and ten degrees. Even along the Gulf Coast with its "cool" breeze.

"You see the end of that pier?" Jessie asked Cliff, Rachel, Gwen, and Kayla as LucyFur eagerly lapped up vanilla ice cream that was melting down from Jessie's cone. "Remember that one time, Cliff when we came here in high school? I had that cheerleading competition?"

"Yeah, what about it?" Cliff answered.

"Well, remember that cute little burger joint we ate at?" Jessie continued. "The one where I bought that little tank top, hoping to get some action from you? That's where it used to be. Now it's the end of the pier. That's how much of the beachfront the ocean has swallowed up in the last several years. I mean, this is crazy at how fast this shit's moving. Coastlines getting flooded by the oceans. Extreme droughts in the Midwest. Off the scales hurricanes and tornados. Mother Earth is *really* pissed. And *now* it's payback time. If only our parents' generation had had enough balls to do something about it when there was still time. But nooooo. They had to fight just to keep our democracy from falling to the autocratic fascists. They were too busy trying to protect people's right to vote and trying to keep military weapons off of the streets and trying to protect individual liberties from the White Christian Nationalists.

"And that battle still wages. Here we are in the middle of it, trying to find Arima's evil father. But there is one thing that's good so far on this leg of the trip, I suppose. I have yet to feel any pure evil. Oh, sure, I get little twinges every now and then of people who may be sympathetic to those who are pure evil. Their pawns. But *they* aren't *inherently* pure evil. They're just easily brainwashed dullards that don't have the capacity to reason their way out of a paper bag. They just act on impulse and emotion and do whatever they think will get them what they want in that moment. They are ignorant and they are greedy. But they aren't pure evil. And dammit, I'm itching to try out this incantation. I really want to find out if it works".

"Yeah," Cliff interjected. "They're kinda like *your* followers used to be. Just mindlessly taking your advice. Of course, your advice wasn't to try to overthrow the government or oppress other people or anything like that, but I bet a certain percentage of them would have jumped on that bandwagon if you had told them to".

Jessie glared at Cliff at the suggestion. Then her expression softened, and tears formed in her blue eyes as she absorbed his revelation. "Wow, you're right. It was so *easy* to get those people to buy *anything*. Even stuff that I knew sucked. It didn't matter to my hardcore followers. You're right. I could have told them *anything* and they would have done it, without thinking about it. Jesus, when did so many of the people in this country become so simple? So self-absorbed? Or maybe they always have been. Maybe there have *always* been a bunch of people who would sell out to anyone and anything just to get what they want. And I kinda played a part in that. I played a part in brainwashing people to believe in me just because of an act I was playing on my platforms. It was all an act. The make-up. The hair. The bubbly personality. I was just performing for them. And they ate it up. I *knew* that I was manipulating them, and I *loved* that I was manipulating them. And I didn't think about how I was contributing to the brainwashing of the masses. I feel really ashamed right now."

Cliff sat next to his beloved wife and placed his arm gently around her shoulder. "Hey, it's okay. We *all* have played a part in this madness one way or another. Maybe we didn't vote. Maybe we didn't march. Maybe we allowed ourselves to become indoctrinated into some mindless cult, like, well…I guess I've just been thinking about *my* upbringing. *My* religion. I've been questioning about how my entire religion just sat there as children were being raped by priests. They were raping children and creating more and more rapists from their congregations. For generation after generation after generation, so many of these innocent victims were so messed up that they became molesters as well. And what did my church do? Pope after Pope after Pope? They just moved the rapists around. Moved them to a new hunting ground, so they could rape a new batch of kids. They intimidated the victims and did everything they could to not take any responsibility. The congregation would just pray that it would stop. Well, how did that work out? How many kids were being raped by their priests at the *very moment* that congregations all over the world just sat on their hands and prayed. I don't know, Jess. If that's what it means to be a Christian, then…I guess I'm not one. But I *do* believe in Jesus Christ. I believe in the inherent goodness and acceptance of others in his teachings. I just don't think that *any* religion that would allow those horrible things to happen is very Christ-like. Something changed in me that night that I snapped that guy's neck. It's all fine and good to turn the other cheek. It's all fine and good to pray. But I think that Jesus wants us to actually *take action* when we need to. He wants us to *take action* to protect the vulnerable from the truly evil in this world. My church should have turned those horrible priests over to the authorities as soon as they found out about what they were doing. But they didn't. They tried to cover it up. And why? For their own self-interest. So that they wouldn't lose any of their flock. So that the collection plates would continue to fill up so that they could buy more priceless artifacts and build fancy churches. It's disgusting, and I'm pretty ashamed of myself, too. So I've also played *my* part in this madness. That's all that I'm saying. C'mon, the Triplets are getting impatient."

"C'mon you guys!" Gwen yelled out to them from the open window of their RV. "We're almost out of dough! We gotta get to the casino and restock the coffers!"

It is said that there are two absolutes in life: death and taxes. Actually, there is a third absolute. Vices. Regardless of the economic times, political upheaval, or personal situations that may be happening, people will always find a way to search for satisfaction within their own personal vice whether that be junk food, tobacco, drugs, liquor, sex, or…gambling.

As LucyFur was purring next to a battery-operated air conditioner in the RV, Jessie, Cliff, Rachel, Gwen and Kayla were strutting into the casino located in Galveston. They approached an elderly woman of Japanese descent who was sitting at a slot machine pressing buttons. She pressed one more button on the machine and red lights went off. "Jackpot!" the woman exclaimed as she pressed *"Cash Out"*, took her receipt, and turned to leave.

She pivoted from the operant conditioning device and saw five smirking faces. "Oh, my darlings! It is soooo nice to see you!" she exclaimed as she was enveloped in hugs. "Well, I've just about tapped this place out. I'll hit two more slots, then shoot some craps for a while, then retire to my comped suite. Oh, won't you stay the night? My suite has plenty of room and there's an Eighties hair metal tribute band playing in the lounge tonight. It will be sooooo fun, and I haven't seen you all in soooo long!"

"We would be honored," Gwen replied as Kaneko squealed in delight, "Wha-wha-whaaaat? You'll stay? Oh, how marvelous! Come, let's play a bit of poker then. Let me show you my magic touch!"

Kaneko's family name meant "Golden Child." Her parents could not have predicted the future impact of her given name. Once she was given the name Kiaria, the dye for her future abilities had been cast. Together, the name Kaneko Kiaria meant "Golden Child that is Fortunate." And she was. In spades. And hearts. And clubs. And diamonds.

Kaneko had been lucky for all of her life. When she was a child, she never lost a board game or game of cards. Ever. She would always draw the exact card or roll the exact number on the dice that she needed to win a contest. As a teenager, she slipped and took an unfortunate spill off of a diving board only to land directly into the outstretched arms of a handsome lifeguard. He became her first love. When she was of age, she began buying lottery tickets. It was as though she could sense exactly which ticket in the spool held the greatest payout, whether it was within the first ten, fifty or hundred tickets. She would purchase the required number of tickets, take them home and scratch them off. Inevitably, there would be a jackpot. Then, there were the state lotteries. She would wait until a particular lottery was built up, then buy one ticket. She could imagine the winning numbers in her head. And she would win in state after state after state. She became a multi-millionaire and invested much of her winnings in stocks and bonds. Her portfolio never lost a dime. When she was in her thirties, she met Louise Azar, who was one year younger. The pair became the best of friends, and Louise marveled at Kaneko's gambling prowess. It also didn't hurt their friendship that Louise never had to pay for dinner or entertainment. Money was no object to Kaneko. Anything that she might need at any given moment was only a casino away.

Louise asked Kaneko if she would like to be introduced to the other members of her sosyete, to which Koneko replied, "What in the hell is a *sosyete?*"

Louise, answering through her chuckles, responded. "Well, the literal definition of a sosyete is a voodoo congregation. Now, our little group of ladies isn't so much about voodoo, although there are some that dabble in it. We adopted the name because we are a congregation of women with special abilities, and we combine our strength to protect ourselves and those that we care about. And I care about you and with your special golden touch, I believe that you would fit in wonderfully."

Kaneko was introduced and felt immediately loved and welcomed by the diverse group of powerful women. They taught her that her special ability was not just for her own use but could be used to help others as well. Although all of the ladies in the group were financially self-sufficient, it did not hurt to have a fortunate benefactor in their mix to bankroll the costs of special assignments. Special assignments like finding a purely evil pastor who was trying to usher in the Age of Vetis, for example.

Kaneko began accumulating wealth not just for her own purposes. She began to distribute that wealth to others who were less fortunate than her. She would donate money to help victims of a violent storm re-build or relocate. She paid for numerous expensive medical procedures for those who were shut out of the American capitalistic health care system. She bought presents for the less fortunate at Christmas and school supplies for all of the area schools each September. She found that she loved to give even more than she loved to win, and this provided even more motivation to continue. She was not investing or gambling out of personal greed any longer. She was investing and gambling out of altruism. She was investing in and gambling for humankind.

And what she found to be *most* altruistic was to assist those who had been battered and abused by horrible men. She would listen with grave seriousness to the plight of a woman who was being abused and had no way out. She grieved with the women as they told her how they were simply unable to leave their abusive partners out of fear for the safety of themselves, their children or their friends and family. These were men who were so vile and consumed with power, that they would threaten death upon the women's loved ones in order to keep them under their sadistic thumbs. So the beatings continued. The bruises continued. The rapes continued. The lacerations continued. And the women found themselves in helpless and hopeless situations.

Until they would cross paths with a member of the sosyete, who would refer the woman to Kaneko. As Kaneko would look upon this sobbing, pitiful soul, she would ask quietly, "What do you want to have happen to this impotent worm?" The woman would respond forcefully in a deep, determined voice through her tears and gritted teeth, "I want him to die."

Within a week's time, the problem would be eliminated. Kaneko had become associated with a powerful hitman syndicate who had taken it upon themselves to be freed from the shackles of their organized crime overlords and use their skills to benefit the less fortunate. The downtrodden. Their services were quite expensive, but they had developed a network of benefactors to assist in payment for those who truly needed them. Although the group was based in Brooklyn, they performed their services throughout the world. And they were very effective.

She would place a call with a name, description, and address and the problem would be taken care of. She became a quiet, behind-the-scenes referral source and benefactor for the group and gained great stature in their eyes. Because of this, she was the only person outside of the group to ever know their true name. In the hushed circles of New York's underworld, they were known simply as Murder, Inc. Kaneko held the high honor of knowing them as *vendetta degli oppressi*, or *revenge of the downtrodden*.

Kaneko began leading her friends towards the high roller poker table in the rear of the casino. She looked like a mother leading her eager ducklings to a fresh pool of water. "The trick, my dears," Kaneko began explaining, "is to not stay at any one table or machine for *too* long and not win *too* much. You will see me fold many hands at this table. You will see me lose a number of times, but if I were to play every hand, I would win every hand. Then the big fish will swim away. I will have scared them off. And I don't know about you, but *I'm* in the mood for a grand prime rib dinner and perhaps six bottles of Dom tonight."

True to form, Kaneko folded multiple times. Frequently, she folded a pair of aces. The cigar- puffing men would chortle with greed as they would enthusiastically rake in the chips, hand after hand. They would whisper to each other and wonder why this Asian grandmotherly type was sitting here with her ever-present purse on her lap. Being men, they did not notice that her purse was a designer brand worth nearly $5000.00.

Kaneko would fold yet another hand, then say as she put the next ante in, "Oh, well. Maybe I'll get lucky this time, huh fellas?"

The men would roll their eyes and laugh at her dismissively. About an hour into her arrival at the table, the men's laughing abruptly stopped as Kaneko hit on a bit of a lucky streak. A queen- high flush that beat the ten-high flush. The four eights that beat the four threes. The jack-high full house that beat the four-high full house. The small straight that beat three of a kind. Within ninety minutes, Kaneko had turned $500.00 into $10,000.

"Well, *that* certainly was fun, wasn't it?" she said to the visibly shocked men. "I don't know what got into me. I guess Lady Luck is on my side tonight. You gentlemen have a lovely evening. Oh, and if you're going to go see the band tonight, please come and say 'hello'. I just love to dance! Toodles."

As the party began moving toward the elevators, Jessie said, "I'm going to go out to the RV and get LucyFur. Cliff, could you come along and help with the bags?"

"Of course," Cliff responded as he jumped to attention and followed his wife out the exit and toward the back parking lot.

As the loving pair approached the RV arm in arm, Jessie suddenly buckled over and exclaimed, "Oh Christ, Cliff! There's pure evil here! It hurts!"

In order to try to comfort her, Cliff bent by his wife's side as two dark figures rapidly emerged from the side of the RV and clubbed them in the head.

Cliff and Jessie woke up a few minutes later. Cliff had blood dripping down the side of his head as he looked at Jessie, who was shaking her head violently and attempting to free herself from the ropes around her arms and legs.

"Well, mornin'," one of the skinheads said while wearing a lascivious grin. "So you've been trackin' our boss, huh? Well, now *we're* trackin' *you*. And we're gonna send a little message to our boss's daughter. Yep, it's time that she come out and play. On *our* field. Damn, baby. You are cuyute! Why don't we just start by puttin' that purty lil' mouth of yours to work, huh? While your husband *watches*, heh, heh, heh."

Jessie looked up at the disgusting man as he began unbuttoning his filthy jeans. "Oh, I'll put my mouth to work, all right," Jessie replied in a dark determination. "Malum tuum dolorem facit. et dolor meus es fortitudo mea."

"What the hell did this bitch just say?" the other skinhead laughed out. "Hell, I thought she was American! I guess she's just another foreigner from one a-them shithole countries!"

"What I *said*," Jessie replied tersely, "is in Latin. "And what it *means* is... 'your evil causes pain. my pain is my strength.' And what it means for *you* is that you both are *screwed*!"

Jessie tore out of her ropes with one movement, jumped to her feet, grabbed the nearest skinhead with both hands by his greasy skull, and pulled upward. The man shrieked in agony as his head and spinal column were ripped from his body, creating a geyser of blood that LucyFur drooled over from the RV window. She took the spinal column and impaled the other skinhead from under his chin through the top of his skull. An astounded Cliff sat there in silence as he was showered with pieces of brain, skull, and blood.

"Oh, baby, are you okay?" Jessie stated frantically as she bent over her husband and began straining against his ropes. "Oh, dammit!" she cried out. "I should have left one of them alive for a bit longer. As soon as they both died, I lost all of my strength. Sorry, baby. I'll go get a knife."

Cliff sat in shocked silence and nodded as LucyFur jumped out of the opened RV door and pounced upon the headless body. She began purring contently as she gluttonously lapped up the blood.

"Where have *you* two been? Kaneko asked as Jessie and Cliff approached their friends who were seated at a corner table of the buffet. Seeing that the pair had changed their clothes, she began chuckling and said, "Oh, I think that I know. Well, it took you awhile. Good for you, young man."

"No...it wasn't...um...*that* exactly," an embarrassed Cliff replied.

"Uh, no," Jessie interjected. "Let's just say we ran into a bit of trouble, and I think that it's in our best interest to miss the band tonight. I'll explain in the RV. But before we go, I've gotta find a manicurist."

"Why?" a confused Cliff asked.

An exasperated Jessie looked at him and replied, "Because! Just look at this! I've broken one of my nails! I can't go out in public looking like this! C'mon, Cliff! Let's find that manicurist. You guys finish your dinner, and we'll meet you back in the RV."

"Um, okay," was all that Cliff could say as he trailed behind his determined wife.

Chapter 21

Hey! You Didn't RSVP!

"This shade of pink does *nothing* for me!" Jessie bellowed out as Louise was helping to fix her hair on Valentine's Day 2038. "And I'm pushing thirty! I'm practically ancient! I can't afford to waste a day looking like...like...*this*! And, oh, my God! I'm going to be *photographed* in this pink nightmare!"

Louise and Jamie chuckled and shook their heads at the still youthful and perpetually vain twenty-seven-year-old former cheerleader. "Dearie," Jamie replied as she shimmied into an identical hot pink dress that had a plunging neckline and clung to her body just above her knee. "I picked these bridesmaids' dresses out myself! As you know, Arima really had no interest in making the wedding plans. She just told me to tell her when and where to show up. She *did* take charge of the reception buffet, however. But other than that, I have been *frantically* planning this! Booking Marcus's church! The florist! The photographer! The DJ! The guest list! The wedding invitations! And, yes, the bridesmaids' dresses and shoes. I am *telling* you, girlie, I am just about at my wit's end, so *do not* mess with me! It would *not* take much to make me violent today! You *will* wear that dress. You *will* smile, you *will* be pleasant, and you *will* stop your bitching! Do you understand?"

"Yeah, fine...Sorry," Jessie retreated before asking her friend, "So, are Stellan and Paciano gonna make it for this shindig?"

"Oh, I invited them, and it really isn't like them to miss such a gala event," Jamie began explaining with restored joviality. "But they have *finally* been hired by that sweet family from Brooklyn to restore an old country estate that they have purchased. It had been used as a compound by the local fascists there, but now that the fascists have been...well...*taken care of* in that county, they have purchased it and hired my lovely bears to restore it and be its caretakers. They are *soooo* excited to be back in their home county and to be able to live in such a grand estate. But they said the fascists tore the hell out of the place and they have only two years to get it ready. That is when the couple plan on retiring and showing it to their teenage daughter. Two years from today, in fact. On their wedding anniversary and their daughter's sixteenth birthday. Strange that Arima is getting married on the same day, isn't it?"

Louise stopped curling Jessie's hair for a brief moment as a slight unexplained chill ran up her spine. She then abruptly changed the subject and asked the Triplets, who were doing each other's hair and giggling, "So you have not been able to locate the reviled Pastor, hmmmm? It has been four years. I would have thought that with Jamie's Beholding ability to sense evil and your three's ability to hone in on a particular dark soul, that we would have located him by now. It has been nearly a year since his little piss ants ambushed you at the casino. What do you think is going on?"

"Louise, I'm so sorry, but I honestly don't know," the "eldest" triplet Gwen began explaining in a frustrated voice. "We know that he is able to shroud our tracking ability by hiding behind the symbol of Vetis. That the demonic symbol of Vetis can somehow shroud him. But it *can't* shroud him from Jessie Beholding his true evil. His sadistic essence. She has consistently been able to pick up on that, and we then were able to focus all of our tracking energy upon his soul. But he was always gone by the time we arrived at his latest hiding spot. He always was able to stay one step ahead of us. We had him on the run, at least. We were able to track his movements. That all changed several months ago, right after the ambush. We can think of only two explanations. He either has died and now is in spirit form, which may make him even *more* formidable, or he somehow has learned how to shroud himself from Jessie's Beholding ability as well. To be honest with you, this wedding is a nice break for us. We've been doing this nearly non-stop for four years. We understand its importance, but it's really getting us down. So, we welcome this opportunity to let our hair down, get drunk and get laid! Right, girls?"

Rachel and Kayla began giggling in response, before Kayla said, "You know the type I wanna screw tonight? I don't know why, but I've always kinda been turned on by tall, pale dudes. Don't get me wrong, I love rolling around with a brother, but there's just something about those pasty skinny white boys that turns me on. And if they're blond, so much the better."

"Oh, *me, too*," Rachel purred. "It's almost like we have a white nerd fetish or something. Especially if they have a bit of *bad boy* in them. Respectful to us, of course, but...a bit of a mean streak and not afraid to get their hands dirty. That would be totally hot!"

"You two are *freaks*," Gwen shot back in a playfully disapproving tone before a laughing Louise said, "Well, I'm not aware of anyone that meets that...um...*criteria* being invited to the wedding. I think the closest thing to that would be Clyde, so I suppose you two could fight over him."

Rachel and Kayla looked at each other as they pondered the suggestion before bursting out laughing. "Um...I don't think so," Rachel stated before Kayla included, "Naw...I mean he's a *really* nice guy, especially for a white dude, but he's a bit too old and his hair's a bit too...um...not very much, so...yeah...nope."

"Come, my lad, let me get a good look at you!" Clyde excitedly ordered as Marcus came down the stairs of Arima's home to greet his wedding party. Marcus beamed with pride as he looked down upon Clyde, Cliff, and his Moms and Pops. "Oh, my! That gangster's black tuxedo looks just *wonderful* on you!" Clyde exclaimed. "And look! You can barely see the fifteen bullet holes on the chest and the blood stains are practically non-existent! Oh, how dashing you look, my lad."

"Thanks, Clyde," Marcus replied. "And thanks again for finding this suit. Wow, that was really great timing, wasn't it? You know how nervous I was about finding something nice to wear for my wedding that I could afford. I couldn't find anything, anywhere. And then, two weeks ago, this mobster who is *exactly* my size just buys it outside of the opening of his restaurant. He was a real dick, too. Racist. Womanizer. Woman beater. Scam artist. Arima had no idea where to put his spirit."

Marcus then let out a roaring laugh as he continued his story. "So...oh, man, I can't tell this with a straight face...Arima knew that he would never get into Enlightenment, and she didn't want his spirit hanging around, so she wanted to get rid of him. This dude hated Mexican folks, right? So she put his dark spirit into a pound of hamburger, cooked him up, and put him in tacos. She ate *all twelve* tacos, then…well…let's just say that several hours later, she flushed him away."

"Well," an astonished Marcus's Moms replied as his Pops was bent over in laughter. "Your new bride is certainly getting…um…*creative*, isn't she? Well, she is your perfect match, it would seem, and she has been so good for you. We absolutely love her, Marcus, and we are *so* proud of you today. We are proud of you *every* day, but *especially* today. There aren't a lot of men like you and your father around. Men who treat women with respect. Men who don't see women as subservient to them, but as equals. Men who aren't running around chasing everything in a skirt. There aren't many of you and I am *so* proud to be the wife of one and the mother of another. And we just *love* Arima. As if she were one of our own and we will be *so proud* to call her our daughter-in-law in just a few hours. Come here my son and give your parents a hug."

Following his emotional embrace with his parents, Cliff approached Marcus and placed a purple iris boutonniere on his lapel. "Congratulations," Cliff said with a slight tear in his eye. "I am so happy for you today. And I am so happy for my friend. I've known her for so long and she is such a kind soul. It just warms my heart to know that two of my favorite people in the world will be united today. I love you both. And I've seen Arima's dress. You're going to be blown away, dude."

―――

"Oh, my God! Why aren't you *dressed* yet?" Jamie screamed at Arima who was lying on her bed in her stained pajamas while watching an old *Twilight Zone* and eating glazed donuts.

"What's the big deal?" Arima responded casually. "I just gotta put on my dress. We don't have to be there for, like, I dunno, two hours or something."

"Arima," Jamie coolly responded through gritted teeth as she folded her arms. "Are you *baked* right now?"

"Well, y'know…um…not much. Hey. Have you tried these donuts? They are like the greatest donuts in the history of the world. *Soooo* good…" Arima's thought trailed off as she took another large bite and slowly began chewing with a look of pure ecstasy on her face.

Jamie took in and then let out a deep breath before continuing. "Arima, I love you. But I have worked and worked on planning this wedding. For you. For my best friend. And *not only* do you need to put on the dress, but we have to do your *hair*. And your *make-up*. And I think you *might* just want to shower, seeing as how this is your *wedding day*. And no, we do *not* have two hours. We have *forty-five minutes* before your ass is to march down that aisle. So you will please forgive me when I say to you... put the donuts *down*, get off of the *goddamn* bed, get in the *shower* and get dressed!"

As Arima and her wedding party were about to depart for the church, a sobering Arima heard a sing-song voice in her soul. *Arima...Oh, Arimaaa....Aren't you forgetting something?*

"Ah, shit," Arima said out loud as she approached the painting of the Jamaican harbor. "Yeah, sorry, Howard. Okay, you can come along. Come on into my soul. But be on your best behavior or I'll put your old ass into the cake and eat you! Got it?"

Yeah, yeah, I got it, a disappointed Howard replied. *And have you invited the others? Will they be there?*

"Yeah," Arima answered. I've prayed for the attendance of Becky Peterson and her two daughters, Lillian, Herbert, and Iris, and their little adopted spirit daughter, and of course, the Ropers. They'll all be there."

Good, Howard replied with satisfaction. *I have a feeling that their presence will be important today.*

Marcus nearly passed out from a sudden rush of blood from his head to his other head as he saw the most beautiful vision of beauty being escorted down the aisle by Louise. Arima looked absolutely radiant in her dark purple strapless wedding dress. Her breasts were fighting against the soft fabric to remain in place as her long, flowing ruffled train followed behind each step that she took to the cadence of the wedding march. Light purple Zinnia petals appeared from nowhere and gracefully landed upon the carpeted aisle in front of her as Arima and Louise heard Lillian giving quiet instructions to two giggling young white sisters and a twelve-year-old Black girl.

Arima looked down upon her ring and saw the hazy image of a smiling

Becky. As she approached the altar, all of the perfectly bloomed bouquets of purple iris stood perfectly upright, and their sweet scent filled the room.

The congregation observed a joyous Louise give her beloved granddaughter a long embrace. She held Arima's tender face in both of her hands and said quietly, "I don't know how long that I will be with you on this earth, but I am so happy that I have lived to see this day. Today is the day that you will truly take your place in our long line of strong Azar women. Today is the day that you will grow up and completely see your destiny. Today is *your* day. And *nobody* can take this from you. I will always love you, my dearest child." Louise then took her seat next to Marcus's parents in the front pew. The congregation was unable to see what Arima then felt. They were not able to see Mr. and Mrs. Roper give Arima a light kiss upon her forehead before floating to the back of the church.

Arima's tear-filled eyes looked up and met those of Marcus. They stared at each other as they lovingly took each other's hands. Their hearts were pounding with pure joy as the pastor began.

"Dearly beloved," the pastor began with a soft sneer. Arima looked up at the face of their pastor. She then watched in horror as she saw his two disfigured hands grab the bottom of his face and lift upwards. Their pastor's face was removed to reveal the bloody face of her father...the Pastor.

The Pastor began cackling as everyone heard the church's doors being slammed and locked. Standing behind them were eight skin-headed, brown-shirted, fascist hooligans carrying assault rifles.

"Just calm down, everyone," the Pastor said haughtily to the now-panicked crowd. "Just take your seats and maybe, just *maybe*, *some* of you will make it out of this alive. Oh, my darling daughter. You didn't forget to invite your dear old dad now, *did you*? Oh, I wouldn't miss *this* blessed event for *anything* in the world. Oh...well...perhaps world *domination*, but this is a step towards that now, isn't it? I'll tell you what. You just come along with me now, and I'll spare everyone else in this damnable church. Even your bitch grandmother. Or you can try to fight me, and they will all experience a horrible death at your side. Your choice. Tick-tock, my little bundle of joy, *heh, heh, heh*."

"Wh-why can I not sense you? Why can I not sense your evil?" Jessie blurted out.

"Oh...*that*," the Pastor responded arrogantly. "You see, I grew tired of our little cat and mouse game. And I grew tired of painting the symbols of our glorious Vetis all over the walls of whatever shack that I was forced to hide out in. They didn't stop *you*, anyway. So I needed something stronger. I needed to physically sacrifice for Vetis so that he would shield me from you. So…heh, heh, heh…I did *this*!"

The Pastor cackled wickedly as he removed his robe. There was a collective gasp as ever-widening eyes viewed the seventy-five-year-old lanky, naked frame of the Pastor that was covered in deep scars. Every inch of his body was covered by the carved marks of Vetis. Every inch except for his bloody face and disfigured hands.

"I am now *invincible*! There is *nothing* you can do to me! My *marks* will protect me! But there is *nothing* that can protect *you* my darling daughter! *Nothing*! And I will now *prove* it to you!"

The Pastor reached behind the altar, retrieved a long sword and impaled the heart of…Louise Azar, who had instinctively jumped to her feet, rushed the altar, and absorbed the lethal thrust.

"Grams!" an anguished Arima screamed. She heard the Pastor yell out, "Now!" Then the *rat-a-tat* of horrid guns launching their deadly projectiles. Nobody but Arima could hear the voice of Howard also yelling out *Now*! And the congregation, both living and spiritual, leapt into action.

The iris blossoms suddenly extended and began enveloping the marauders in their blooms, stems and leaves. The spirits of the three young girls were saying, *Die! Die! Die!* over and over as they used their energy to physically pick up candlesticks from around the church and plunge them into the eye sockets of three of the attackers. Lillian and Becky streaked from assassin to assassin, spinning them around and making them disoriented as Mr. and Mrs. Roper lifted various crucifixes and drove them into their blackened hearts.

Jessie softly uttered her incantation and rushed into the hailstorm of bullets alongside the knife-wielding Gwen, Rachel, and Kayla, as Cliff and Marcus grabbed as many of the members of the congregation as they could and led them out a side exit to safety before quickly returning to the battle. Jamie ran up to one of the iris-bound men and thrust her hot pink, spiked stiletto heel repeatedly into his groin while shouting, "Am I woman enough for you *now*, Father? Well, *am I*? Is this *macho* enough for you? Are you proud of me *now*, you bastard?" She looked the man in his dead eyes, took the weaponized shoe off, and flung it across the room, spraying the deplorable's blood and semen on its journey to the far wall.

Arima's tears were falling into the wide-open eyes of her deceased grandmother as she heard the voice of Louise say, *It's all right, my dearest.* A brilliant blue light slowly lifted from Louise's deceased frame and grabbed the Pastor by his left wrist. Another brilliant blue light emerged from inside the stained-glass window and grabbed him by his right wrist. Arima's mother, Abdalla, smiled at her as she and Louise lifted the Pastor three feet off of the ground. The Pastor began screaming, "What are you *doing*? You can't *do* this to me! I am *invincible*! Oh, glorious Vetis! Why have you *forsaken* me? Why have you…"

Arima then saw a third brilliant blue streak stand in front of the man and begin chuckling.

"Who…Who are *you*?" Arima asked the spirit, who turned his ethereal and brawny frame towards her and said in a mischievous voice, *Let's just say I'm a friend. I'll let you take care of this douchebag, and I know that I wasn't invited, but I just couldn't resist having a little bit of fun, heh, heh, heh.*

The Pastor began screaming out, "No! Not *you*!" as his fingers were meticulously snapped one at a time for the second time in his life. Following the final cracking sound from the Pastor's pinky, the third blue streak turned to Arima and winked. *Have fun, kid. I have a feeling we'll meet again sometime.* Then, he floated away as quickly as he had arrived.

The Pastor struggled in vain to free himself from the tight frigid grasp of Louise and Abdalla as they placed him on a large crucifix at the front of the church. The Ropers each grabbed a hammer and nails and pounded his re-disfigured hands and scarred feet to the cross as he screamed in agony.

Arima turned around and viewed the carnage that this demon…her father…had wrought. She saw the blood-soaked forms of Jessie, Cliff and Jamie holding each other while sobbing uncontrollably.

She saw Kayla and Rachel holding the head of Gwen between them in their laps. Gwen's brains were oozing out of her exploded skull and saturating their hot pink bridesmaids' gowns. She saw Clyde. His suit was beyond repair. As was his riddled face. And she saw Marcus with his fists clenched standing over the mutilated bodies of his parents. She then knelt down by her grandmother's body, gently closed her eyes and righted herself.

She glared directly at the Pastor and said with a deep resolve, "You son of a bitch. *Why*? What is *wrong* with you? All of this *pain*. All of this *suffering*. All of this *death*. For *what*? *Money*? *Power*? What *is* it that you hoped to *get* out of all of this? What goes on in your head to get such a *thrill* out of oppressing others? *Manipulating* others. *Murdering* others. *Raping* others. *Destroying* others. Destroying them *physically*. Destroying them *mentally*. Destroying them *emotionally*. Why? Because someone *looks* different than you? They don't believe *exactly* like you do? They don't *love* like you do? Anything that is *slightly different* from you has to be *destroyed*? *Why*? And how do *you* know that you are the one that is right? Maybe it's the Jamaicans who are the master race! Maybe it's the Hispanics! Or the Asians! Or the Buddhists, or Muslims! Maybe it's just women in general. Or maybe it's the transsexuals or lesbians or gay guys! Maybe it is. You don't know! You just use your white, faux-Christian, male privilege to convince others like you that *they* should be dominant over others. That they have the *right* to destroy others. Well, you don't. None of us do. None of those groups are any better or any worse than any other. We just want to live a happy, normal life without being *exploited* by corporations or politicians or clergy or pundits. Without being *gunned down* in our schools or churches. Without being *abused* and *assaulted* and *raped* and *murdered*. Is that too much to ask? To just treat each other with respect? To support one another and help one another to be happy? And not *despite* our differences, either. To support one another *because* of our differences. To support one another because we embrace and love other people because they *are* different from us. Look at you, writhing in pain, nailed to that cross like some sort of holy martyr. *You*, and *everyone* like you who uses religion to brainwash people into hating others are not Christ-like. *You* are the exact opposite. *You* are the anti-Christ. Spin this bastard!"

The spirits of Louise and Abdalla spun the cross so that the Pastor and crucifix were now inverted. Arima took the sword from her grandmother's still heart with certainty and turned toward the anguished Pastor whose blood was rushing to his face from his upside-down frame.

He began pleading using his most convincing slithery voice. "Please, Arima. Y-y-you are right. Of course, you are. But you are too *good* to do this. I *know* that now. *You* are not a killer. You are *good* and *kind* and..."

The Pastor's words were cut off as Arima said in a frigidly calm voice, "Oh, shut up, you manipulative, con-artist, slimy piece of shit." The Pastor's head was removed from his body with one violently smooth swing of Arima's arms. His head rolled and landed on the outstretched hand of Louise's body. A waterfall of blood flowed out of the Pastor's lifeless body, creating a crimson river that flowed down the carpeted stairs through the center aisle and seeped out of the bottom of the closed front door.

A dark purple, cackling plume emerged from his decapitated body. *Oh, you think that you have won now, do you? I will be even more powerful now! I have made the ultimate sacrifice and am sure to be in the favor of our glorious Vetis! I shall still see you destroyed, my darling daughter! Only this time, I shall find my way into your soul! I shall...*"

The Pastor's threats were silenced as his mouth was covered tightly by a large fig leaf. Then his essence was enveloped by that of Lillith. And the twelve-year old spirit that Lillith had avenged. And Becky. And Becky's young daughters. And the Ropers. And the Botanist. And Iris Rose. They encircled and bound the Pastor before being joined by the spirits of Clyde, Gwen, and Marcus's parents. The Pastor's muffled screams could be heard as his dark form was lifted up and out of the church.

Arima looked upon the final two spirits. She looked into the angelic eyes of her mother and grandmother. She smiled at them. They smiled back. The spirit of Louise then said, *It is my time, my dearest. My time to go to Enlightenment with my daughter. And we, along with the others, will keep that heinous man from you. We will protect you from him. We will leave these others for you. They are weak and you will be able to dispose of them as you please. Your father, however, is very powerful. We must protect you from him. But you must play your part. There is only so much we can do. If you get too close to him again, he may be able to penetrate you. He may be able to control you. Especially if he is in league with the copperhead. Please, my dearest. Stay here and protect your loved ones. Stay out of New York. C'mon, Howard, let's go.*

M-me? Do I get to go with you? an emotional Howard stated as he emerged from Arima's body. *Thank you, Arima. We will all be looking over you. Maybe there truly can be redemption for even the most darkened soul. If we allow ourselves to let go of our hatred towards others. Our pride. Our greed. Our lust. Maybe we can all be saved someday. Thank you for showing me that Arima. Thank you for giving me the opportunity to be someone decent. Good-bye.*

Arima watched with mournful ease as the final three brilliant blue streaks ascended out of the church toward Enlightenment.

Everyone in the room remained silent as Arima sploshed through the blood and collected each of the remaining eight dark souls that were attempting to hide from her. One by one she would capture them, then place them in the holy water font at the front of the church. She heard their desperate cries as their essence were being burned by the blessed liquid. Once the final dark soul was in its place, she lifted the font to her lips and drank deeply. Every drop. She wiped her mouth, belched, and said, "Well, it worked with the tacos, so I suppose this should work, too. I'll be right back. I gotta take a piss." She opened the bathroom stall and found the body of the church's true pastor. His throat was slit, and his face had been peeled from the skull.

Arima returned from the restroom and looked at the man who remained her fiancé. She broke down in tears once again as the weight of this tragic day fell upon her bloody, bare shoulders. Marcus wrapped her in his massive arms. He concentrated with all of his might. He concentrated on absorbing her pain. Her loss. And she concentrated on absorbing his. And at that moment, they realized that they did not need to have a ceremony to be wedded to one another. At that moment, their two souls became one.

Chapter 22

Woo Girls and Nuptials

On the morning of February 14, 2039, Marcus and Arima simultaneously woke up with a start. They wiped the drool from their respective chins, looked at one another and said in unison, "Do you wanna get married today?"

"Whoa," a startled Marcus stated. "What the hell is going on? I mean, I just had this dream where my Moms and my Pops were telling me...well... telling me..."

Arima completed his sentence. "Telling you *and* me that we needed to get married today. Officially. That this day can't be about mourning their loss. They want it to be a celebration of their lives. And the lives of the *others* that we lost that day. Clyde. Gwen. My Grams. That it is to be a celebration of their lives through being a celebration of our love for one another. And a celebration of defeating an evil man, whose sprit they have locked in confinement somewhere in the darkest corners of Enlightenment. Yeah, they said the same thing to me. I can connect with them directly when they allow me to. Apparently, they can come to you in your dreams. Kinda like that copperheaded bitch, I suppose. And I haven't heard from her in years, so I think I'm all clear on that front. Maybe she's been locked away, too. Or destroyed. I dunno. All that I know is that I think that I'm rid of her and my dick of a dad. So I think that I agree with your Moms and Pops. Let's do it. And let's do it right! You're the manager of the morgue now, so you can take off whenever you want. And as your employee, I would like to request the next two days off, all right? Let's get the gang together, fly to Vegas, get drunk, get stoned, and get hitched!"

Marcus burst into joyous laughter as he rolled on top of his beloved and began kissing her passionately. Twenty-three minutes later, they picked up the receiver of their avocado green rotary phone and began making their plans.

"Fine!" Jessie yelled into the receiver. "But I am *not* wearing that pink nightmare again! It's got blood and shit all over it, anyway. Cliff! Call the folks that you're working with and tell them that you need a couple days off! Family emergency! We're going to Vegas! And go upstairs and get Kayla and Rachel up! They're coming too! And LucyFur...get off the counter! Um...or don't. It's okay. I guess you can be up there. Good kitty. Just be cool. Okay, Arima, we'll see you in a while."

Arima shook her head and chuckled as she placed the receiver back in its place. "Okay, let's go tell Jamie."

Since the passing of her grandmother, Arima had inherited her home and the group's living arrangements had changed. Marcus and Arima lived in her grandmother's home along with Jamie. Jessie and Cliff moved into the home of Marcus's parents that he now owned, and they opened up their new house to Kayla and Rachel.

Through their tragedies, the seven friends had become inseparable. This was partially due to their mutual enjoyment of each other's company and partially out of survival. They dubbed themselves, jokingly, *The Seven Saints*, as none of them were *really* very saint-like in their various extracurricular activities. But they *were* quite serious about their motto. They would gather, lift their glasses for their first drink of the evening, and declare, "Strength in numbers!" They vowed to look over one another and protect one another. They vowed to never leave anyone behind. And they vowed that none of them would ever be taken down by the hands of evil.

As Jamie was rushing around the house frantically packing and repeating, "Oh, what will I wear? What will I wear? What will I wear?" Arima was staring at the beautiful painting of the Jamaican harbor with Marcus standing behind her.

"Y'know," Arima stated with a hint of sorrow, "I miss everyone so much. Your Moms and Pops. Gwen. Clyde. My Grams, of course. And I even miss Howard. He was such a big dick, but he became a part of my life, y'know?"

"Yeah, I know," Marcus softly replied as he wrapped his arms around her from behind. "But just look at what you did with him. You took a miserable soul who had committed the most horrendous atrocities and, over time, showed him how to care about others. You gave him the chance to redeem himself. And that's really special. *You're* really special."

"Yeah, well," Arima replied as she began to snicker. "Grams visits me from time to time in my dreams. So does my mother. Anyway, they told me that Howard's life, if you can call it that, in Enlightenment isn't *exactly* what he had hoped. They said that he was there on the condition that he is the eternal servant of all of the souls that he had abused when he was alive. So he spends all of his time running around from soul to soul getting them drinks, rubbing their feet, and pretty much anything that they want him to do. He did find some chick's spirit that is into pegging though, so I guess he has *that* going for him."

"Man," Marcus stated as he physically recoiled from his love. "Why didja have to mention *that*? I don't wanna picture some female spirit giving it to Howard up the ass! Next time you hear something like that, just keep it to yourself, okay?"

"Okay," the laughing Arima replied as they heard the honk of a car horn outside. Jamie rushed out the door with her three suitcases, followed by Arima and Marcus who were sharing a small carry-on. Arima locked the front door, turned around and saw a thirty-foot white stretch limousine. Rachel and Kayla were hanging out of the sunroof with bottles of champagne and yelling, 'Wooo!' repeatedly for no known reason. Jessie was yelling at a nervous-looking Cliff outside of the car and saying, "What do you *mean* you didn't pack it? Why wouldn't you *pack* it? Do I have to tell you *everything*?"

And Kaneko was raising her glass while exclaiming, "C'mon, bitches! We've got a wedding to get to! Get your asses in the car and let's go party!"

"Hey, driver, turn here please," Arima instructed a short while later. "We have one stop to make before we go to the airport."

The Seven Saints and Kaneko delicately placed vibrant bouquets of flowers upon each grave of their departed loved ones. They all said a silent prayer at Clyde's grave before Marcus placed a motion-detector dancing skeleton upon his headstone. They began walking away, and the skeleton began laughing and dancing. "That's how I will always remember him,"

Marcus stated quietly. "Laughing. He was dry as hell and his jokes were so bad, but the man loved to laugh."

They placed another bouquet at the base of Gwen's black marble headstone. Rachel and Kayla, who were now referred to as *The Twins*, embraced and told a brief story about their fallen sister. "Y'know, Gwen was so funny," Rachel began. "She was always so protective of us. She was like a mother hen. Always scolding us. Always beating up anyone who bullied us in school. She appointed herself as our leader. And why?"

Kayla then answered while chuckling. "Because she was our *older* sister, heh, heh, heh. *By thirty seconds*! She popped out first and from that moment on she took it upon herself to mother us, I guess. I mean, she wasn't any smarter than us, right?"

"Well," Rachel quietly replied, "She *was* always the one that had the coolest head. She was more calculating than us. Less likely to act on pure emotion. We need to learn that from her, sis."

They moved on and were enveloped by the shadow of an eight-foot-tall granite sculpture of a Jamaican woman with an angel's wings. Her soft face peered down at her granddaughter as Arima placed the large bouquet of color in the sculpture's outstretched hand. Arima looked up into her eyes and swore that she saw a single tear fall from the granite. The entire party held hands as Arima said, while fighting back her tears, "Awww, shit, Grams. The things that you d-did for me. My entire life. You taught me how to be a good p-p-person. You never gave up on me. You guided me without y-yelling at me. You protected me from evil. You helped me learn how to use m-m-my abilities. Y-y-you truly loved me. Hell, you even d-died for me. I l-love you Grams, and I just cherish your visits with me in my d-dreams. But it's not the s-same, y'know? You're n-not there anymore to bake me your delicious c-c-cookies or to scold me when I'm b-being irresponsible. It's just not the s-same. But it is special. I l-love you, Grams, and I always will. I will t-try to make you p-proud. Thank you." A single bird flew to a nearby tree and began singing. Arima looked lovingly at it, smiled, and winked away a final tear.

"Why don't you all go back to the limo," Marcus suggested as the group made their way toward two modest headstones. "I kinda want to do this one myself, if that's okay."

"Of course, it's okay," Arima replied with a soft understanding before placing a light peck on her love's lips.

From the nearby limo, Arima watched her love kneel between the rose-colored granite headstones. He placed the bouquet between them, then a picture of his proud parents holding their infant son. He lowered his head and began sobbing. He then began laughing loudly, looked up to the sky and said, "Yeah, okay. I won't. I understand. I'll make ya proud of me. I love you both and, yeah, I'll visit."

Marcus entered the limo and looked upon the other seven grief-stricken faces. "Man, I don't know about all of you, but I *really* need to get baked."

The limo pulled up to the curb of the airport. The chauffeur got out, went around the lengthy vehicle and opened the side door. Billowing smoke came tumbling out, as did Kaneko, who landed on her side, then rolled over to sit on the sidewalk with her legs splayed open. She was laughing hysterically, as were the other seven revelers.

"Man, are they even gonna let us on the flight like this?' the ever-worried Cliff asked to a response of renewed laughter.

"Just be cool. Just be cool. Just be cool," was all Arima said repeatedly as they stood in the airport security line. The security guard looked at each member of the party, their ID's, and their boarding passes. He giggled slightly and said, "Vegas, huh? Well, that seems appropriate for you folks. I'm not sure you need a plane to get there, though. Looks to me like you all could fly there yourselves. Well, have a good flight. And remember! No smoking in the terminal or on the plane!"

"We won't, officer!" Kayla playfully replied before saying, "Hey. You're kinda *cute*. You wanna come with us?"

The tall, blond, pale young man stammered, "Ummm..yeah. I mean...um, no, ma'am. I have to work and stuff. But maybe when you get back...um... maybe..."

The disheveled young man was cut off by Rachel who said, "Nope. You had your chance. C'mon, sis. See ya!"

The young man had difficulty holding his attention on the next passenger as he heard one of the identical twins saying, "I *know* he's cute, but we can't *both* have him. I don't think. Don't worry. We'll find a pair of pasty-faced albinos to play games with at some point. I can feel it in my... well...let's just say that I've got this feeling."

The eight slightly sober friends followed Kaneko to their luxury suite. She opened the doors and exclaimed, "Welcome to paradise, kids! Marcus, you and Arima have that bedroom over there and your suit is waiting for you. Arima, I have your dress in my room, over here. Cliff and Jessie, you two take that room. And, sorry, folks, but Jamie, Rachel and Kayla will have to share. But if any of you need a little more…um…*privacy*, here are keys to three regular rooms on the twenty-third floor. Order what you want! Eat what you want! Drink what you want! You want a stripper? Get one. You want a massage? Get one. You want a full lobster dinner just to take one bite of? Get it! Who cares! Money is no object! Tonight, you are with Kaneko!"

"Wow," Jessie stated in wonder. "We *really* need to hang out with her more often." She then sheepishly inquired, "Soooo, what if one of us - and I'm not saying *who* - but one of us sees a pair of designer shoes?"

Kaneko burst out in laughter, embraced Jessie, and whispered into her ear, "Tonight, my dear, you will live like a queen. Get whatever you want. There are no limits."

Jessie's knees began quivering as she breathily ordered, "C'mon, Cliff. Let's check out the bed!"

"Uh, okay," Cliff dutifully replied. "But I'm sure it's fine. This is a *really* swanky place and I'm not really all that tired and…"

He was abruptly cut off by his wife who screamed, "Oh my God! You are so *dense* sometimes! Just get in here and screw me!" So, he did.

For the second time in his life, Marcus nearly passed out from the vision of beauty that was his Arima. He stood there in his brand new black designer tuxedo and watched his bride-to-be glide down the aisle in her full-length purple gown that was covered in beautiful green hibiscus blossoms. He took her hands and shed a tear as he peered upon her lovely face. They then looked intensely at the face of the wedding official. Arima could sense that others were doing the exact same thing at that moment. The Ropers. Lillian. Becky and her giggling daughters. Herbert, Iris and their adopted daughter. Louise. Gwen. Clyde. Abdalla. Marcus's parents. And… Howard.

Pull on his face Arima! I don't trust him! Howard bellowed out. *And make this quick. Don't take any chances this time. Just say your 'I Do's' and get the hell out of here!*

"Why are you in such a rush?" Arima's soul said to Howard's. "You got a hot date or something?"

Yeah, I actually do, Howard replied mischievously. *You know that woman spirit that's into pegging? Well, she just conjured up a new toy that she wants to use on me, so…*

"Howard! Shut the hell up!" Arima's soul yelled out as she could hear the laughter of all of the other spirits, with the exception of one. *Mommy, what is pegging?* Arima heard the voice of a young girl inquiring. *Never you mind, dear. Arima, let's get this thing going,* came Becky's terse reply.

"Okay, just a standard Elvis," Arima stated, following her intense inspection. "Let's go. Marcus, this was supposed to happen one year ago, and although that was...um...interrupted, that doesn't make this moment any less special. I love you and I want to spend my life eating with you, getting baked with you and rolling around in bed with you. You cool with that?"

"Yeah, sure am. Ditto," came Marcus's enthusiastic, albeit short response.

"*Ditto?* Is that *it?*" a slightly annoyed Arima asked.

"Yup, ditto," came Marcus's playful response. "What else do you need me to say? I mean, I'm starving, so what else is left?"

"Yeah, nothin', I guess," Arima answered through her chuckles. "And I'm starvin', too. Okay Padre or King, or whatever. Let's make this shit official!"

The rest of the evening was taken up by visits to two buffets, one fast food taco joint, a dispensary for another kind of joint and twelve bars, four of which they were *very* overdressed for. Their intoxicated heads and staggering bodies made their way back to their suite. Except for Rachel, Kayla and Jamie, who took new "friends" to private rooms on the twenty-third floor. As they were waiting for their limo to take them to the airport the following mid-morning, they recounted some of the previous evening's highlights. The specific names that are attributable to these quotes have been redacted based upon the "laws" of Las Vegas and shall always remain in Las Vegas.

"Worst wedding vows ever!"

"You did *what* in the bathroom?"

"I really didn't think that it would fit! But you know what? It did! Wooooo!"

"Then I opened my mouth and I..."

"Oh, my dearies! The look on that man's face when he looked up my skirt! It was a look of sheer delight!"

"Cliff! Hurry up with those bags! And don't drop the one with my new shoes!" (Okay- that one is Jessie)

"So then I said to him, why don't you stop talking and do something *else* with your pretty little mouth? So he went under the table and he..."

"I really didn't think that he would be that flexible. But you know what? He was! Wooooo!"

"No, I swear! I didn't get...um...y'know...hard when she was doing that on my lap! I swear, Jess!" (Okay- that one is Cliff)

"Hey, I think you got some sour cream on your shirt."

"That isn't sour cream, dearie."

"So, once I was able to talk again, I said to him, 'Fine. You can stick it in there. But if you're not done in five minutes, I'm calling it a night!'"

"That might have been the most beautiful evening that I've ever spent with anyone."

"Yeah, me too. Those were the greatest buffets in the world. And the pot was pretty good. Not as good as mine, but it was okay. Oh, and our wedding night. That was great, too, baby."

Marcus and Arima flopped down on the sofa in their living room, looked at each other's exhausted faces and began laughing.

"Damn, baby!" Marcus stated through his chortles. "Now *that's* how to get married! Maybe we should do that again *next* year for our anniversary! And, man, those twins are wild! Get a few drinks in 'em and they're like ravenous tigers or something! I mean, how many dudes did they bang anyway?"

At that moment, Arima noticed the flashing red light on their answering machine. She pried herself off of her cushion and dragged her feet across the room as she said through her laughter, "Yeah, that was great, and those chicks are super fun. But if I hear 'wooooo!' one more time. Hold on a sec. I gotta check this."

Arima pushed *Play* on the answering machine and heard the panicked voice of Stellan. "Oh, Arima. This is Stellan and Paciano. Could you please call us back as soon as you get this? Thank you, sweetheart."

"Huh," Arima stated. "I wonder what that's all about?"

She dialed the phone and heard Paciano's mournful voice say, "Yes, hello?"

"Hey Paciano. It's Arima. Sorry I missed your call, but we've been in Vegas. What's up?"

"Oh, sweetie, only the *worst* thing *imaginable* has happened!" Paciano began through his tears. "That *sweet man* who has hired us has been murdered! *Just last night*! *Stabbed in the back*! His poor wife is just *beside* herself I have heard. Oh, and their *poor* daughter. To lose her daddy at *only* the age of fifteen. And on her *birthday*, no less! We haven't met the darling yet, but I just *so* want to go to the city and give her a big bear hug! I'm sorry to bother you like this. I don't know why I called *you* right away. It was like I had this little voice in my head that said 'Call Arima. She can help'. Oh, my sweet, I don't know how you can help, and this sounds all so silly, but I just think that if you came to New York, then…well…maybe things would be better somehow."

"Oh, man, Paciano, I'm so sorry," Arima sincerely replied. "I would *love* to come to New York to help, but I just *can't* right now. I just took two days off to get married and I've got tons of other stuff going on. I'm so sorry. But how about this? Marcus and I were just talking about what to do for our one-year wedding anniversary. How about we lock it in? We will be in New York exactly one year from now to celebrate our anniversary and to meet your friends that you've been talking about. Okay?'

"Yes, yes, of course that would be wonderful," an understanding Paciano replied. "Just wonderful. One year from today. It will be so lovely to have something to celebrate rather than mourn. One year from now. February 14, 2040. It is a date."

Arima hung up the phone, turned to Marcus, and said, "Well. I guess we have anniversary plans. We'd better tell everyone to see if they want to go. Right after I get baked and take a nap. Then, maybe a snack. But I'm *definitely* calling everyone after that."

Chapter 23

Sister Act

There was a noticeable strut as the seven friends walked towards the baggage claim at LaGuardia, and with good cause. It had been a good year. The number of evil souls that they had all encountered, battled, and destroyed continued to dwindle. Their deceased loved ones kept them apprised of the Pastor's continued confinement. And there was no sign of the sinister copper headed demon. The forces of fascism continued to be beaten back in county after county in the United States, and they were playing their part in defeating the deplorable minions of Vetis. They had cause to be confident. They had cause to be happy. And once Kaneko arrived with Stellan and Paciano, there would *definitely* be cause to party on this Valentine's Day of 2040.

Upon reaching the baggage claim, Cliff dutifully watched for their bags as Jessie and Jamie went to the restroom to fix their faces. Kayla and Rachel giggled and scanned the crowd for potential love interests while periodically shouting 'wooo' for some unexplained reason. And Marcus and Arima stepped outside for a much needed "break."

As they were passing their joint between them and snickering, a large stretch limo pulled up to the curb. "Well, hello bitches!" Kaneko yelled out from her perch in the sunroof. "Get the other bitches and let's go shopping!"

Stellan and Paciano tumbled out of the limo, rushed up to Arima and

Marcus, and gave them tight bear hugs. "I...can't...breathe," was all that Arima could utter through her crushed diaphragm.

"Oh, I'm *soooo* sorry, sweetie!" Paciano declared. "It's just so *good* to see you both! Welcome to New York! It is gonna be hot in the city tonight!"

"Yes, it is!" Stellan enthusiastically agreed. "Once everyone gets assembled in the limo, we'll go over the plans for the day...and the night. And, Kaneko, it is so wonderful to meet you. Thank you *so much* for picking us up at the estate."

"Oh, you're welcome, fellas!" Kaneko shouted out. "And thanks for the tour of the place. That mother and daughter will be so happy there. And you've both done such a wonderful job restoring it. And it is so cool that your friends are the same people that are my associates here in New York. What an incredibly small world! I was just so shocked when I saw the family portrait hanging above their fireplace."

The remaining revelers jumped in the limo as Cliff helped the chauffeur load the bags. Once everyone was present, Kaneko began. "Okay, kids, so here's the plan. We're going to go get checked in at our hotel and drop this shit off. Then I've got a little...um...business to conduct with some associates that I have in Brooklyn. It shouldn't take too long. They have an IT whiz there that has been doing some...um...research for me and I just need to check in with him, and the boss of the joint, if she's around. But if not, I'll see her tonight, as it very pleasantly turns out. Gee, it must be my lucky day...ha! So, you kids are all going to be dropped off in a shopping district in Brooklyn. Here's a credit card. Buy whatever you want."

Jessie began trembling and said breathily, "Oh, Kaneko. I don't know that I've ever loved *anyone* as much as I love you right now." Jamie was visibly amused. Cliff was visibly displeased.

"Yeah, yeah, yeah, it's okay kiddo, my pleasure," Kaneko laughed in response. "So, we'll get together at six o'clock for dinner and drinks and then the main event. We will all be going to a fancy nightclub for a huge blowout. And finally, the *Seven Saints* from New Orleans and Murder, Inc. from Brooklyn will come together at last for a night of unified frivolity!"

Kayla and Rachel looked at each other, smiled, jumped up through the open sunroof, and began yelling "Wooooooooo!".

"Here, hold this bong and these rolling papers. Oh, and these donuts," Arima ordered Marcus, who was standing outside with Cliff, watching the blur of activity from shop to shop of their female counterparts. "Hey, man.

Look at this sweet new coat I got. Isn't it just the most beautiful shade of purple? Here, hold my old one. I wanna wear this new one. It makes me feel regal or some shit."

"Cliff!" Jessie then commanded. "Here. Hold these shoes. And *these* shoes. And *these* shoes. And these dresses. And this purse. And *these* shoes. Thanks, honey!" Following a quick peck on the cheek, Jessie was once again a blur.

Marcus and Cliff just looked at each other and shrugged. "Decent weather today," Cliff suggested.

"Yeah, pretty normal February day in the mid-forties in New York, I guess," Marcus replied as he shook his head. "Man, I remember not that long ago when there would be *blizzards* in New York in February. And now, it's like early Spring. Yeah, but there's no such thing as climate change, now is there? Dumbasses." Marcus then saw the ride of his dreams come screeching around the corner and pull up to a very abrupt stop near the local pet store.

"Hey, Arima!" Marcus yelled to his wife who was across the street. "Check out this sweet ride!"

Arima looked to where Marcus was pointing and began drooling. Arima had possessed no interest in owning a car in her life, but the vision in front of her was a hippie's wet dream. It was also the wet dream of Kayla and Rachel, who saw two tall, pale young men emerge from the back. They were identical twins and had long blond hair and wore matching all-white suits.

"Oh, *hello...*" Kayla purred before Rachel added, "Oh, *yes...*come to Momma. Or come *on* momma. Whatever you *want.*" Their excitement subsided when they saw a young blonde woman and a young African-American man emerge next. "Eh, *she's* probably not with them. And *he* isn't, either. I'm pretty sure they're single. And if not...well...they wouldn't be the *first* entangled guys that we've seduced," Rachel said confidently to a nodding Kayla.

Arima walked toward the vehicle as if in a trance. It was a completely restored 1976 VW bus. Its bright yellow paint glistened in the sunshine. There were randomly placed seventies-style flowers of multiple colors and sizes painted on the body. The passenger windows had multicolored beaded curtains that could be closed when the bus was not being driven. It was the epitome of utopian hippie freedom. It was the epitome of a symbol of peace. To Arima, it represented hope and friendship and love. She also thought that it would be the absolute best vehicle in the history of the world to get baked and laid in.

Two nearly identical women then emerged from the front of the van. The only discernible difference between the two was that the driver was at least twenty years older, and her copper-auburn hair was straight while the younger of the two had curly copper-auburn strands. But they were both short, had the exact same facial features and blazing green eyes.

The younger one got out of the passenger door, slammed it and yelled, "Mom, I *love* you, but sometimes you drive me *crazy*!"

The driver began laughing and said, "I love you too, sweetie. I *know* that I drive you crazy because I'm the one *driving*! Get it? Get the play on words? Hey! How come you're not laughing? That was *gold*! Pure fuckin' go—"

And then...all hell broke loose. Arima heard Jessie behind her scream in anguish, "Oh, my God! The pain! I've never felt such pain! Such evil!" There was a hail of gunfire, and the driver of the van was struck multiple times. Her petite body was flung eight feet backwards from the torrent of lead and she landed harshly on the cracked concrete.

From her peripheral vision, Arima saw Marcus and Cliff on one side of the street and Jamie, Kayla and Rachel on the other begin directing innocent bystanders to safety.

"Mom!" the younger woman cried out as she rushed to her mother's side and took her hand.

As did Arima. She ran as fast as she could, with her dark purple coat flying behind her like a cape. She reached the woman and held her other hand. She looked into the sobbing green eyes of the daughter, then down at the fading green eyes of the mother, who was gasping for air and spitting up blood as iron-scented, crimson molasses began pooling around them all.

Arima then heard the voice of the blonde female assassin. "I *told* you, bitch! I fucking *told* you that I'd get you back!" Arima looked up and saw the woman standing fifteen feet away, holding a smoking assault rifle with an expression of absolute glee on her face. "Oh, they all said that I was *crazy*! But they were *wrong*! Could a *crazy* person manipulate an attendant in a psych hospital into helping her escape? Could a *crazy* person frame him for the murder that she herself committed? That's *right*, bitch! *I'm* the one who stabbed your fucking husband in the back! Just like you *both* stabbed *me* in the back! I took him from you, and *now* I'm taking your worthless life!"

Arima became frozen in absolute fear as she heard the assassin's voice change. It changed to something even darker and more sinister. It changed to the voice that she had heard on her twenty-third birthday. *And we're going to take the life of your precious daughter, too. Hello, Madeline, I should thank you for waking me by desecrating my grave. You awoke me, and now I have come for my revenge. You were always such an ungrateful little whore. And now, I am sending you where you belong. All I needed to do was find a human vessel who hated you as much as I did. And I found her. And I entered her body. And I can live here forever and emerge whenever I choose. And now, before you die, I want you to watch as I send your daughter to Hell with you.*

Arima screamed at her body to move. To do something. But her psyche was too absorbed by absolute terror to do anything but watch as she continued to hold the hand of the fallen woman. She watched two pale, blond young men approach the assassin, say something to her emotionlessly, then calmly snap her neck.

A dark, shadowy cloud of filthy, purplish smog emerged from the assassin's warm corpse and looked down upon the carnage that it had created. It began to chuckle before a bright white cloud enveloped it. The two forms were swirling in and around each other in a billowy blur of entanglement. They looked like two curtains being whipped against one another in a violent windstorm as brilliant flashes of dark purple and brilliant light blue flashed in an epic war. The two forms savagely collided one final time and merged into one. There was an impossibly high-pitched, tormented shriek, and the battling shrouds dissipated as quickly as they had arrived.

The dying woman gave her daughter a slight smile as her eyes faded from green to grey. The daughter cried out in tortured loss. She was lifted from the blood-soaked pavement by the pale twins, a young African-American man and a young blonde woman. They escorted the inconsolable young woman away. Arima did not know why she felt such a bond to this particular woman. She had seen others die in front of her. She was always filled with remorse for the needless loss of an innocent life. But she had never felt it like this. This sense of loss and remorse penetrated her to her bones. This sense of loss and remorse penetrated her very soul.

And then she felt something else. Something much more familiar and comforting. She felt the dead woman's spirit. She was not gone. She had not been allowed to enter Enlightenment. Arima began silently reaching out to the woman. *Please, spirit. Tell me your name. Please. I am here to help you.*

The spirit seemed to Arima to either be too shy or too frightened to reveal herself to her.

Arima continued to try to make contact. For nearly five minutes, she continued to hold the corpse's hand and repeat over and over again, *Please spirit. Please tell me your name.*

Arima then learned that the spirit was neither shy nor frightened as she felt the spirit's soul connect with hers. The pair were facing each other soul to soul and were now two souls in one. Arima then heard the annoyed voice of the spirit say forcefully, *My name? My name's Maddy* fuckin' *Sommers! Who the fuck are you, bitch?*

TO BE CONTINUED IN *PURPLE REIGN: HANGING CHADS BOOK IV*

"Hey! Hold up a minute! Don't stop reading yet! Sorry for the interruption, but my name's Maddy Sommers. You just met me and..."

"Um...hey...Maddy? What're you doin'? I mean, the book's over and I think that I've earned a little down time after this. I just want my husband, a bong, and some potato chips. And donuts. And maybe a frozen burrito. Or two. Oh, and a pizza. Since I'm in New York, I *have* to try their pizza and..."

"Yeah, yeah, yeah, the fuckin' pizza's great here, Arima. But I've gotta talk to these readers for a minute. I mean, you have totally bogarted this *entire* fuckin' book! I got what...maybe *three fuckin' lines* in this whole thing? And I'm the fuckin' *star*! So, if you would *pleeeease* allow me to continue without interruption? Thank you for your cooperation in this matter. It is truly appreciated."

"Anywhoooo...as I was saying before I was so *rudely* interrupted, if you thought that this was just a one-off story that was not connected to a series, well...SURPRISE! It *is* connected to a series! My author thought that this might be a fun way to reach out to new readers and attract them to the series, but he doesn't know what the fuck he's doing, so what does he know?"

"Anyway, we all hope you enjoyed this little story. Not sure how you could, seeing as how I'm *barely* in it, but I digress. If you liked this, then the story will be continued in *Purple Reign: Hanging Chads Book IV*. But if you haven't read the first three in the series, you will have no idea *what* the fuck is going on. So, I encourage you to pick up *Hanging Chads, Lineage: Hanging Chads Book II* and *Ascension: Hanging Chads Book III*. Then, you'll be all caught up. And those three books are *waaaaay* better because they're all about lil' ol' me. Y'know, my upbringing and what drove me to be a vigilante serial killer, then falling in love and getting involved in a hit man syndicate, then having a kid and becoming a freedom fighting serial killer. Then there's all the stuff about my parents. That shit's pretty fucked up. It is packed full of violence, blood, gore, profanity, humor, societal discussion, and romance. Y'know. Typical stuff. So pick 'em up and I'll see ya in those pages! What do you have to lose, *heh, heh, heh*. Lata, Gatas! Maddy out!"